# Princess BMX

## marie Basting

**Chicken House**

2 Palmer Street, Frome, Somerset BA11 1DS
www.chickenhousebooks.com

First published in Great Britain in 2019
Chicken House
2 Palmer Street
Frome, Somerset BA11 1DS
United Kingdom
www.chickenhousebooks.com

Cover and interior design by Helen Crawford-White
Cover and interior illustrations by Flavia Sorrentino
Typeset by Dorchester Typesetting Group Ltd
Printed and bound in Great Britain by CPI Group (UK) Ltd, Croydon CR0 4YY

The paper used in this Chicken House book is made
from wood grown in sustainable forests.

1 3 5 7 9 10 8 6 4 2

British Library Cataloguing in Publication data available.

PB ISBN 978-1-911490-94-4
eISBN 978-1-912626-42-7

*For Mary Girl*
*and*
*the three generations of radical*
*dudesses she inspired.*

*Always in our hearts, Nan xxx*

Trust me, the fairy tales have it so wrong. Dingy towers and wicked stepmums are the least of my worries, it's the boredom that will kill me. Sure, there are worse things than being a princess. I mean, it's not like I have to shovel dragon dung for a living. But, honestly, apart from the endless supply of cupcakes, being a princess is pretty rubbish.

There are *certain expectations* as my dad is always telling me. Ridiculous expectations like sticking my pinkie out when drinking tea and never needing the toilet in public. How can I not need the toilet with all that tea? Then there are the princess lessons. *Like, ugh!* The hours I've spent walking around balancing a blancmange on my head, you wouldn't believe it. Seriously, being a princess is so dull I used to think about locking *myself* in a tower and throwing away the key.

Thank the good goblin then for potato sacks. Because if I hadn't been sliding down the stairs in a potato sack, I'd never have discovered the portal. And if I hadn't gone through the portal, I wouldn't have got my BMX. And if it wasn't for BMX nothing would have changed . . .

# CHAPTER 1

The day everything changed started out like every other day. I was in trouble again. I shut my eyes, but it was no use. When I opened them Dad was still there in the Grand Hall with his nose curled up like he'd just stood in something nasty. I call this his troll-poop face. He pulls it a lot. Today, as well as pulling the troll-poop face, he was doing the finger wag. The finger wag means I'm in real trouble.

I sighed and climbed out of the potato sack I'd been sliding down the stairs in. My silver shoes clacking on the mosaic floor, I traipsed across the Grand Hall to where Dad was standing in his fur-trimmed cape next to a polished suit of armour. *Clack. Clack. Clack.* My footsteps sounded out my doom. I was *so* in for it now.

Dad looked at my crumpled gown and shook his head.

'Whatever next, Avariella!' he said, taking his pocket watch out of his waistcoat and flicking open the lid. A tiny red cuckoo popped out of the watch face.

'You're late,' it said.

Dad took a deep breath. It seemed ages before he let it out again. 'You were supposed to be ready ten minutes ago. What do you think you're doing, sliding down the stairs in a vegetable sack?'

I smoothed down my pink gown and gave him my best puppy-dog eyes – you know, the wide-eyed cute look that's always a winner with grannies? Well, it wasn't a winner with Dad.

'And don't look at me that way!' he said, wagging his finger again. 'I was very clear with my instructions – we must arrive at the Bubblegum Bazaar before the crowds.' He pressed his lips together and shook his head. 'Really, I don't know what I'm going to do with you.'

This was a lie because he clearly *did* know what to do with me. He did the same thing he does every time I'm in trouble, which is send me to my chambers. Originality is not one of Dad's strong points. Mind, I can't talk because I did the same thing I do whenever he grounds me. I pulled a sad face and made my way slowly up the stairs.

Oh, don't worry, I was only sad on the outside. Inside I was like yay, oh yay with unicorn bells on! I mean, what a result. What's the point of travelling miles across the kingdom to a fete when you're not allowed to join in with the fun stuff anyway? Much better to stay home sack-racing. But first I needed to make sure the coast was clear.

I flung open the door to my room, kicked off my sparkly shoes and zoomed round the four-poster bed to the window. The second sun was rising and the sky was streaked with pink and orange. I opened the window and breathed in the sweet scent of chocolate blossom that grew in Biscotti all year round.

Ooh, as well as having his best togs on, Dad was taking the fancy gold carriage. He was standing in front of the four white horses with my brother, Bertie, waiting for Mum. Bertie's satin knickerbocker suit was the same shade of turquoise as the horses' feathery headdresses. As for Mum's latest fashion disaster, she looked like she'd borrowed her outfit from Little Bo Peep.

She had Doreen tucked under her arm. The micro-unicorn's long mane was brushed perfectly straight and the pearlescent bump, where her horn was yet to grow, glistened in the sun. Dad glared at Mum. It didn't matter how cute Doreen looked with her gold-painted hooves: there was no way she was getting in the carriage with them. Last time we took Doreen with us on a royal visit, she bit the Earl of Bourbon and weed on his wife's shoe.

Dad wagged his finger at Mum – yep, I wasn't the only one who got the finger wag! She put Doreen down and, laughing, shooed her back towards the palace. They all climbed into the carriage and the coachman cracked his long leather whip and pulled away. I waved, but they didn't wave back.

Sighing, I shut the window, tracing the route of the carriage on the leaded glass as it left Castello di Cannoli and raced across the draw-bridge. Through the pink haze, I could see far across the kingdom: the colourful gingerbread houses and shops of Amaretti town; scattered villages formed of thatched cottages and farms; the stinky swampland where the giant ogres live; and far off in the distance, on the other side of the Black Forest, the cornfields and rolling meadows that lined the Limonadi River.

The carriage was almost at the edge of town now. Some kids about my age chased it up the street. I turned away, fighting the familiar empty feeling in my chest. There was no point wishing. *A princess is not expected to play with her subjects.*

Oh, whatever. It was time to get my potato sack back. And with the servants given the day off to go to the bazaar, this time nobody was going to ruin my fun.

# CHAPTER 2

I don't want to sound like a show-off, but I'm brilliant at sack-sledging. It's all in the position. The lower your body the faster you go. Making sure I was sitting under the chandelier that marked the exact centre of the grand staircase, I climbed into my sack and popped the cushion I used as a bum protector into place. I pulled the rough fabric tight around me. Ready. Steady . . . Go for it!

Yay, a most excellent take-off. Tugging the sack, I lifted my feet and flew off the bottom step hitting the floor with a thump. *Whoosh!* I sped past the stuffed grizzly bear and through the waiting area, lined with long wooden benches, until I reached the giant free-standing candelabras. There, I twisted the sack to the left and prepared for impact. *Boom!* Right on target – my feet hit the door to the ballroom with a thud and it creaked open.

Mmm, what was that smell? It was sweet like toasted marshmallows. I climbed out of the sack and poked my head around the door. My puppy, Sir Jeffrey Bobbersons – Jeb for short – was standing in front of the marble fireplace which was decorated with the unicorn emblem of Biscotti.

'Stop licking the hearth, Jeb.' I scooped him up and hugged him, ruffling his long, dark curly fur. Yes, a curly-haired dog! I'd never seen one either until Mum gave me Jeb on National Jelly Bean Day. He's a very rare breed though nobody seems to know what it is.

'What has she dressed you in now?' I said, straightening the mahoosive pink bow on his collar. His T-shirt was pink too. 'Party Time' said the slogan on the back.

Jeb woofed and laid a sloppy kiss on my nose. *A princess is not expected to let an animal lick her face*, but like anybody could resist Jeb. Plus, he wasn't just a dog, he was my best friend – my only friend, thanks to Dad.

What *was* that marshmallow smell? Whoa – a weird purple mist was oozing from the fireplace.

'Cool,' I said. Mum and Dad must have decided to go ahead with the Bubblegum Ball this evening after all. Marshmallow mist, what a great way to decorate the room—

There was a frantic bleating sound – a bit like a drowning goat – and something hit my shin: Doreen.

'Careful, Do-Do,' I said, putting Jeb down and extracting her head from my petticoat. 'Go on, shoo.'

Doreen bared her goofy teeth and butted me.

'I mean it. Out of here before you get me into even more trouble.'

Doreen is only allowed in certain rooms in the

castle because, according to Dad, 'she's a ruddy liability'. She is pretty clumsy. I mean, microcorns are cute, but they were at the back of the queue when brains were handed out.

'Help me, Jeb,' I said. 'Get her out of here.'

Jeb woofed at Doreen and they pootled off, Jeb's nails clicking on the parquet floor. He woofed a warning, but Doreen still managed to bump into the birdcage stand.

'I am a potato,' said the startled midnight mynah bird.

The animals in Castello di Cannoli were not the brightest. Good job I had Jeb to rely on. He was always there for me, no matter what.

The mist was thicker now, the smell of marshmallow so strong I could almost taste it. I ran my fingers through the shimmering haze and stuck my tongue out. Tiny drops of sweet marshmallow fizzed in my mouth. Arms out at the side of me like maypole ribbons, I twirled round and round in the sparkly party mist. It was so totally cool, like bouncing about inside a giant violet candyfloss . . .

Erg, or maybe not . . . it was now more like being swallowed by the stuff. The sugar stuck in my nose and throat and made it hard to breathe . . . Oh my giddy goblin, I was drowning . . . drowning in a sea of candyfloss! I had to get out of there. I stumbled towards the door.

And I mean literally stumbled. Suddenly, I was on my knees, my palms pressing against a cold, smooth surface. The fireplace – I'd tripped over the fireplace and landed on the hearth. I pushed myself up . . . That's when I saw it: the mahoosive hole where the grate should have been. I swished the fog away to get a better look. It was like peering through a telescope: in the distance, beyond the tube of darkness, there was a perfect circle of light where I could see blue sky, grass, a river and buildings . . . It was just like being in the palace watchtower looking down across the kingdom.

Only this wasn't Biscotti I could see. There were way too many buildings. Thousands of them, packed tightly together along the banks of a curiously straight river. My heart beating like fairy wings, I thought about the stories

Great-aunt Maude had told me about bad magic – bad magic that never ends well for princesses. I edged away from the hearth.

There was an excited bark behind me. Claws clicked on the wooden floor and a bundle of black fluff emerged from the fog.

'No!' I shouted.

But it was too late. Jeb ran straight towards the fireplace and jumped into the hole.

# CHAPTER 3

OK, thinking about it, following Jeb into the hole probably wasn't the most sensible thing I've ever done. But I didn't get a chance to think about it. Jeb jumped, I followed, and next thing I was sitting on the floor in a patch of weeds waiting for my tummy to catch up with the rest of my body. Like, what had just happened? I felt as if I'd been fed through the laundry mangle, twirled around and spat back out again.

I poked my head above the weeds and took a look around. My neck hairs prickled. Where in the name of the good goblin was I? The river I'd seen through the hole was in front of me. It was dirty and covered in algae. On the opposite bank there were some tall, rectangular houses with flat roofs. Cool, but like totally strange.

'Jeb, are you OK?' I called. 'Jeb?'

My heart was going to burst out of my chest – I couldn't see him anywhere. It didn't exactly look like ogre territory, but you never knew . . .

'Jeb—'

And then I saw him. He was sniffing around under an arched bridge. The bridge was covered in weird paintings and people had written their names all over it in big letters. It must have been some kind of charm or something. It gave me the shivers.

'Jeb, come here, boy,' I called.

Jeb lifted his head but then ran off down the flat paved riverbank.

Growling griffins, that puppy of mine was spending too much time with Doreen. I picked up the hem of my petticoat and legged it after him. He stopped sniffing and wagged his tail, but when I tried to grab him, he ran towards a black-and-white signpost, where he stopped and did a wee. The sign pointed to somewhere called King's Cross. *Panic over!* The king of the realm was bound to know Mum and Dad.

'All right, princess,' a voice called to me from a pea-green boat covered in pots of flowers. *Princess?* Maybe the person on the houseboat knew Mum and Dad. I picked Jeb up and stepped towards it.

I stepped back again. The voice belonged to the scariest man I'd ever seen. The sides of his head were bald, and he had a line of green spikes running from the back of his neck to his forehead. He stared at me, wearing the same quizzical expression as Bertie when he's studying advanced algebra.

'You all right, luv?'

Oh my giddy goblin, one of his teeth was made of gold. Yes, I know, gold! Honestly, I'm not making this up.

'I'm fine, thank you,' I said.

'Been to a fancy-dress party, have we?' He

pointed at my gown.

Fancy dress? What was with this strange man? My dress had been made by the finest tailor in Biscotti. But I didn't bother to tell him that. I figured someone wearing a ripped vest and trousers held together with safety pins probably wouldn't care.

Plus, I wasn't allowed to talk to strangers unless I was with Mum or Dad. I continued along the path.

'Wait,' he called out behind me.

*Unlikely.* This was one of those occasions when even Dad wouldn't expect a princess to remember her manners.

There weren't as many houseboats now, instead the path was lined with tall, flat-fronted buildings with metal balconies. Some of the buildings were covered in weird drawings like the bridge: a purple skull, an eye with a gold crown on it and a giant fist. What did it all mean?

Still, not to worry, according to the signs I'd soon be at King's Cross. I just needed to find the king, tell him who I was and everything would be as cool as a snow-troll with no clothes on. I could tell I was getting close because there were more people about now. It must have been some sort of festival because they were dressed in really weird outfits. *Oooh, maybe there'd be cake!* I trotted along the bank as fast as I could without running. *A princess is not expected to run in the street.*

The path climbed upwards towards a metal footbridge. To my left there was a busy market-place and to the right some shops with tables outside where people sat in the sunshine eating and drinking. Right it was, then. No way was I going through the market. *A princess is not expected to fight her way through the crowds.*

Halfway across the bridge, I stopped. There was a strange humming noise. I stood up on my tippy toes, trying to see over the wall opposite, but all I could see was people's heads and a sign that said 'Camden Lock'. Troll poop, I really hoped I hadn't gone the wrong way. I lifted my skirt tail and scurried past the shops and through the narrow gap at the end of the wall.

# CHAPTER 4

O h. My. Curly. Candy. What magic was this?
A line of metal carriages with no horses
moved slowly along a smooth grey road. I'd
seen pictures of these noisy, mechanical carriages
called cars in storybooks but I thought they were
make-believe. The books said cars could travel
really fast, but these didn't. They crawled along.

And it wasn't just the cars that were strange.
There were shops all around me. They were three
storeys high, but the stuff they were selling was
outside on the street. The shops were painted

20

different colours – purple, turquoise, pink and orange – but they didn't look pretty. Everything was too higgledy-piggledy. The shopkeepers would never get away with that in Biscotti. Not with Dad's rules and regulations.

And why was everyone in such a hurry? Lines of people pounded along the pavement. They were much quicker than the cars, which made zero sense.

'Watch it,' said a girl with short, pale pink hair.

*Like* you *watch it – you're the one who just bumped into me.* But I didn't say that to her. She was far too scary. She rubbed her elbow and blew a strawberry-scented chewing-gum bubble right in my face. She had a silver ring through her nose. Yes, a nose ring like a bull! I repeat, a nose ring like a bull!

I walked on down the high street. It was kind of cool, but, like the girl, everything was really shouty. Music – if you could call it that – blared from a parked car and people hung around outside the shops talking in loud voices. Even the shops themselves had opinions: SUPERIOR

PIERCING AND TATTOO, DON'T MISS OUR UN-
BEATABLE OFFERS, THE BEST FISH AND CHIPS IN
LONDON. None of it made sense.

Jeb whimpered as a car with flashing lights on
its roof made a loud whirring noise. I wanted to
cover my ears but I couldn't put him down in
case someone stood on him. There just wasn't
enough room for everyone. And the smells –
dust, drains, hot chicken – they were making me
feel sick. I needed a minute to catch my breath . . .

Jeb had other ideas, though. He barked excitedly and broke free from my arms. He ran down
the street towards a dog. A dog that looked
exactly like him! It would have been cool, only –
and you're *so* not going to believe this – the dog
belonged to the scary man from the boat. He
picked Jeb up with one enormous hand and
smiled.

'Cockapoo?' he said in his funny accent.

*How frightfully rude.* I reached up for Jeb, and
cuddled him close to me. That man should take a
look at his own dog before calling mine names.
In its studded-leather waistcoat, the poor thing

looked like it was about to go into battle. And it was far too interested in the ruffles of my petticoat for my liking.

The man smiled and grabbed his dog by its spiky collar. 'That's not fancy dress you're wearing, is it, Your Highness?' He winked and took a black rectangular object out of his pocket. He swiped his thumb over the rectangle and it lit up.

*Magic!* Powerful magic like I'd never seen before. I stepped to the side of him and legged it down the street. *Sorry, Dad, but those princess rules just weren't working for me today. It was run or ruin.*

'Hey,' the spiky-headed man shouted. 'Stop. I can help you.'

Like that was going to happen. I ran as fast as I could, wearing a gown and carrying a wriggling fluffball that kept licking my face, but the man followed me. And, yikes, he was catching up. I decided my best chance was to hide. But where? I was so obvious in my bright pink dress.

I took a deep breath and darted across the road in front of one of the slow-moving cars. People poured out of a building with a sign on it saying 'Underground'. I flung myself into the centre of the crowd and walked back the same way I'd come. The spiky-headed man stopped – his head darting from side to side like a dragon hunting its prey. Now was my chance. I stepped sideways out of the crowd and legged it down a side street. I ran. And ran. And ran.

# CHAPTER 5

*C*antelowes Gardens. I had no idea how I'd got to this place that looked like a public garden. I'd just kept running, weaving through the side streets and back alleys hoping to lose the spiky-headed man. Sure, I'd lost him, but I was totally lost too. I was never going to find my way to King's Cross now. And I was, like, totally starving. Perhaps there'd be some toffee apples or cherries on the trees inside I could snack on.

Perhaps not. It was the weirdest garden ever. Just past the entrance, before the sad-looking lawn and crowded picnic benches, sat a grey crater, sort of like a giant's footprint, only the sides of it were smooth and sloped. It must have been dangerous because it was surrounded by a fence made out of chain mail. Not that the fence stopped the kids.

There were two of them. They had these strange wooden boards with little wheels on them and were riding up and down the sides of the crater shouting things at each other like *gnarly* and *sick*. The one with straight dark hair poking out the bottom of his helmet was called Ollie. I know this because the other shouted '*Nice Ollie*' at him when he flew into the air on the wheely-board. Ollie needed to pull his shorts up – I could see his underpants poking out the top.

Jumping jelly beans, what was that? I stepped aside to make way for the strange mechanical contraption that whizzed around me and screeched to a stop outside the crater. Like, no way, it was a bicycle. Of course, if cars were real, why wouldn't bicycles be real too?

I put Jeb down on the floor and followed the bicycle over to the crater. The rider, a girl wearing a shiny silver helmet, must have been important because the wheely-boarders moved out of the way. They huddled against the fence, laughing and chatting. I so wanted to join in but *a princess is not expected to waste her time on trivial matters like making friends.*

The tallest wheely-boarder smiled at me. He had boingy hair that sprang outwards in tight spirals. I smiled back but he turned away before I could think of something to say. This is what happens when you're not allowed to go to school – social skills are so not my strong point. I can, however, embroider my initials on to a handkerchief in less than fifteen minutes. So that makes up for it – NOT!

Ignoring the hollow feeling in my chest, I distracted myself by watching the bicycle. It wasn't noisy like the cars, but it was definitely mechanical. The rider used her feet to wind up the pedals and make it go faster. Oh. My. Curly. Candy. What magic was this? She rode up the slope and flew high into the air, raising her arms out to the side like wings. Without even a wobble, she grabbed the handles again and spun her bicycle round, landing in the centre of the crater.

Everyone seemed really happy about the girl's flying trick. The wheely-boarders whizzed over to her, cheering. They thumped their fists together and talked super-fast, waving their arms in the air.

Clutching the fence, I stared at the flying girl and her bicycle.

I had to try this.

I was too busy watching the girl to notice the second bicycle approach – the screech of the brakes made me start. Jeb barked and jumped up at the rider, a boy wearing tight trousers and boots made out of tent material.

'Sorry.'

'It's cool,' said the boy, stroking Jeb's head. He had a dimple in his left cheek, just like me. 'I've seen her before,' he continued.

'I don't think so. We're not from round here. And Jeb's a boy.'

'Oh.' The boy raised his eyebrow. 'It's just the bow—' He looked at my dress and stopped. 'Friendly little thing,' he said. 'Cockapoo?'

*Really!* What was it with this place? I gave the boy a Dad-style disapproving stare and turned back towards the girl on the bicycle. *Like, wow!* She flew up into the air in front of us and lifted her feet off the pedals. Knees bent, she held the handlebars steady and spun the frame of her bicycle. Round and round it went like a spinning top.

'Nice,' said the boy.

'Oh my giddy goblin, what magic is this? Is it the girl or the bicycle that's charmed?'

The boy pulled a face that made his forehead crinkle. His blond eyebrow looked like a question mark.

'Is your bicycle charmed too?'

The boy still didn't answer. He stared straight ahead at the girl. Maybe he didn't hear me. I should speak louder – everything here was loud.

'Growling griffins, she's amazing. I like her sparkly helmet. Back home, only the knights wear helmets.'

The boy continued to ignore me. Maybe his hearing wasn't great? I stepped closer. His bicycle looked older than the girl's: the paint had faded and the black bits on the end of the handlebars were worn.

'Can your bicycle fly too? Can I have a go?'

He sighed and finally looked at me. 'Dude, how old are you?'

'A princess is not expected to reveal her age.'

He put his hand to his face and shook his head

like something really bad had just happened. When he spoke again his voice was softer. 'Look, I'm going to do you a favour. Maybe where you're from, pretending to be a princess and talking make-believe is OK but, I won't lie, round here it's going to get you in trouble.'

I edged away from the boy. What was he talking about?

'Don't get upset. I mean, it's cool that you're into role-play games and magic, but, well, it's a bit out there. You know what I'm saying?'

What was his problem? I just wanted to know more about the bicycles. Was it really that crazy to think they were magic when the girl was flying around like that?

Obviously, yes. The boy pointed at his head. 'Are you OK?' he said hesitantly.

Oh my curly candy, he really did think I was away with the fairies. Did that mean everyone else here thought I was crazy too? I clicked my fingers at Jeb, but he ignored me and cocked his leg on the fence.

'Sorry, Jeb forgets his manners sometimes.'

'No, I'm sorry.' Shoulders stooped, the boy ran his finger over a faded sticker on the front of his bike. 'I didn't mean to upset you.' He pulled at his bottom lip and sighed. 'Look, my name's Ethan. The bike she's riding's a BMX. And I suppose you're right in a way – it is kind of magic.'

He smiled, but it was a sad sort of smile.

I wanted to tell him my name too, ask him some more questions about the BMX bike, but the words jammed in my throat like a gobstopper too big to swallow. He already thought I was strange.

'Well, see you then,' he said, wheeling his bike towards the gate.

'Ethan,' called the girl on the BMX. 'Come and show us what you've got.'

This time Ethan's smile reached his blue eyes. He opened the gate and the wheely-boarders stood up.

'What's up, bro,' called the tall boy who looked too big for his board. 'Where you been?'

That hollow feeling again. What if this was it?

The only chance I'd ever have to feel part of something? To know what it was like to have friends who weren't canine.

'Wait,' I said. 'Wait.'

Time stopped as everyone around the crater stared at me. I didn't mean to shout but that was the only way the words would come out. What was I thinking?

Ethan smiled. He leant his bike against the fence and closed the gate again. 'What's your name?' he said.

I took a deep breath. 'Avariella. Avariella Petulia Winifred Pandoro D'Allessandro of Biscotti.'

'Right,' said the boy his eyes widening. 'Well, maybe we could just call you Ava?'

'Sure.' *I mean, Ava sounded cool.*

'I'm practising tricks with Cleo right now. But, if you still want to try BMX, come back tomorrow. I'll be here all day.'

# CHAPTER 6

*If you still want to try BMX, come back tomorrow.*

That would be brilliant, yes. But there was a small problem. For that to happen, I had to get home in the first place. I'd been sitting next to the bridge where the fireplace had spat me out long enough to knit a scarf, but I still couldn't work out how to make the mist come back and take me home. I'd tried wishing, jumping up and down while pinching my nose, and saying 'open sesame' three times, but nothing worked.

The King's Cross plan had been a total disaster. Getting there was OK. With Ethan pointing me in the right direction and the black signposts, it was easy to find. Shame then there wasn't actually a king at King's Cross. Nope – you are *so* not going to believe this – but King's Cross was a train station. Yes, I know, cars, bikes, trains, they have them all here. In fact, they seem to have everything – EXCEPT A KING. So much for getting a message to my parents.

Thank the good goblin, I noticed the red mechanical carriages. There were loads of them, lined up outside the station. Just like the carriages at home, they had signs on the front saying where they were going. I scooped Jeb up and sneaked on to the back of the one going to Camden. Easy-peasy, ogres are measly – it brought me right back to the high street.

I might have known my luck wouldn't last. I mean, that thing I said earlier about the scarf, well, it was a lie. I could have knitted two scarves by now. Two scarves, a hat and a pair of mittens! And I'm rubbish at knitting. But anyway, that's not the point. The point is, I'd been here for like ever.

And now it was starting to rain. I mean, it wasn't even a Monday. This place just got weirder and weirder.

'Come on, Jeb.' I ducked to avoid the screeching pigeon that flew from the arch of the bridge towards my head. Ugh, the pigeons in this place were the worst. They were all mangy and dirty. The bridge wasn't any better. I curled up my nose and leant back, placing my foot flat against the wall behind me. *Clang.*

*Like, what?* There was a grid sunk into the bricks. In its bottom right corner was an engraving of a shield. I leant forward and rubbed it, but it was still too dirty for me to see it properly. I spat on my fingers and rubbed again. Yes, I know, disgusting, and not what's expected of a princess, but it was only a little bit of spit and like you've never done it! And anyway, before you get all hoity-toity, wait until you hear what happened next. Because under the dirt there was a tiny unicorn emblem just like the one on the fire grate in the ballroom where Jeb had been licking. I felt a pulse in my fingers and the shield began to glow.

The familiar smell of marshmallows was followed by a violet mist. It oozed through the grille holes and wrapped itself around my ankles. Grabbing hold of Jeb, I shut my eyes and let its cold, wispy tentacles pull me backwards. When I opened them again, I was falling, the gap in the floor I'd been sucked through sealing up until all I could see was darkness – darkness, followed by an explosion of violet light and a whirl of rainbow colours. Still clinging to Jeb, I shot out of the fireplace and slid across the ballroom. We were home.

I stared up at the crystal chandelier and allowed myself to catch my breath. *That was so totally awesome.* I couldn't wait to go back to the Kingdom of Camden again.

Jeb woofed and licked my face. 'You're right, Jeb. We should get out of here before people start arriving back from the bazaar.' The castle was still deserted but it had to be nearly teatime. Dad and co would be back any minute. I glanced over at the grandfather clock: *9.45 a.m?* It must have stopped. There was no way it could still be morning. With Jeb at my heels, I pegged it to my chambers, throwing the door open so hard it slammed against the wall.

*Tick.*

*Tick.*

*Tick.*

The gold clock on the mantelpiece said 9.49 a.m!

*Tick.*

*Tick.*

*Tick.*

I shook it to make sure the hands weren't jammed. I mean, it just wasn't possible. I'd been stood by that bridge in Camden for like ever. I must have been dreaming, or something.

I put the clock down and stuck my face into the water bowl on the washstand. When I resurfaced nothing had changed. The morning sun was still pouring through my window and, according to the clock, it was barely an hour since my parents had left for the Bubblegum Bazaar. The magic that opened the portal was obviously more powerful than I'd thought.

I wiped my face on a gold-trimmed towel, leaving dirty streaks all over the soft cotton. *Eew!* My dress was disgusting too. I took it off and chucked it, along with the towel and my mud-stained shoes, into the snake-charmer washing basket. The black python hissed. I closed the lid and it grew silent again – it's just a hologram, thank goodness!

All the dresses in my walk-in closet are the same – pink, and reeking of Mum's bad fashion sense – so I pulled out the first on the rail. Zipping it up in front of the mirror, I noticed my hair was a total mess too. I picked out the bits of dead grass and ruffled it with my fingers. The Kingdom of Camden really was disgusting . . .

So how come going back again was all I could think about? Going back again and riding on one of those cool BMX bikes. And then there were the cars and the trains and the weird people.

I mean, brill or what? It was just like the stories Great-aunt Maude used to read me when I was little. In fact, I still had the book.

I ran around the bed to the bookshelves. Yes, there it was, my fairy tale collection. Throwing myself down on the bearskin rug, I flicked through the pages until I reached a story called 'The Land That Magic Forgot'. Holding my breath, I ran my fingers over the image of the busy high street lined with cars. It looked just like the place I'd visited today.

*What?* I stared at the frayed binding where some of the pages had been torn from the book. I'd never noticed how the story about this strange 'Other World' suddenly cut off, probably because Aunt Maude never stuck to the book anyway. Maybe it was because the pages had gotten damaged? Or maybe there was something about the story somebody didn't want me to know?

# CHAPTER 7

The five hours I had to wait to ask Aunt Maude about the book were the longest five hours of my life. Jeb had disappeared with Doreen, and there was only so much sack-racing a girl could do. Plus, I was so desperate to find out what had happened to the missing pages, I couldn't concentrate on anything.

Like, where was she? I sat on the sandstone step outside the kitchens waiting for some sign of life from Maude's yellow-and-red gypsy caravan. *Nothing.* Had she decided to go to the

Bubblegum Bazaar? *Mmm, maybe another kip would help pass the time.* With the biscuit-coloured stone warming my back, I lay down on the patio, my eyes wandering towards the fierce gargoyles that lined the castle wall. What was the point of them? If Cook's miserable face didn't scare away bad spirits, nothing would. There was no point to the griffin weathervane on the Central Tower either. The weather was always fine in this part of Biscotti. Except for every second Monday when there was a short rain shower ...

Oh my sherbet fountain, just listen to me. I was so bored! Bored. Bored. Bored. I shut my eyes and, digesting the almond cookie dough I'd pinched out of the larder, watched the orange blotches floating in front of my eyelids. When I opened my eyes again, the first sun was low in the trees by the boating lake and there was smoke coming out of the caravan chimney.

I picked up the fairy tale book and ran down the steep hill, through the rose gardens, and across the croquet lawns to Maude's caravan. The fairy lights were on, and I could hear the pixies singing. Before I'd even climbed the steps on to the lopsided yellow decking, the house sprite opened the door.

'Your Highness.'

He bowed and, spinning across the deck like a tiny turquoise tornado, disappeared. He'd be back as soon as I left, to keep an eye on things.

Maude was sitting in her rocking chair, the heavy lace curtain billowing in the window behind her. Good job the breeze was warm because she was wearing her bathing suit again, the ruffled knickerbockers the same shade of navy as her rubber gardening boots.

'Avariella,' she said, placing her knitting down next to the jam jar that contained her spare eyeball. 'How lovely.'

Aunt Maude never went anywhere without her spare eyeball – she said she liked to know what was creeping up behind her. Yep, Aunt Maude was most definitely a bit short in the marble department. She wasn't always like this. She was once a great sorceress. But something happened to her before I was born. Something nobody ever talks about.

'Avariella,' she repeated. 'Avariella umbrella. Hold on a minute while I find me teeth.'

That was another one of Maude's *things*, as Dad called them. She only ever wore her teeth when she had company – she was worried she was going to wear them out.

'Come in, come in,' she said, scooping her dentures out of a crystal tumbler that was sitting on the side table. 'What are you doing hanging around in the doorway looking guilty?'

As mad as Maude was, she was strangely with it when it came to some things. 'Auntie,' I said, 'can I ask you something?'

'Ask away, but if you want to know why your dad's such a plonker, I have no idea.'

*Like I said*, with it.

'No,' I laughed. 'It's about—'

'Hold on. Aren't you going to say hello to Tyson?'

Tyson is Aunt Maude's pet teabag. He's the reason she got so angry with Dad she moved out of the castle and into the caravan. While everyone else went along with the teabag thing, Dad tried to make her see a doctor.

'Hello, Tyson,' I said, leaning into his cage.

Tyson was sitting in his miniature deckchair, a tiny bobble hat resting precariously on top of his perforated pyramid head.

'He's a bit quiet today,' Maude said. 'Do you think he looks off-colour?'

Tyson looked like he always did. Like a tea bag.

'Maybe he's worn himself out on the hamster wheel,' I said.

Maude poked Tyson with her knitting needle. 'That'll be it. Cage was creaking most of the night, now I think about it. Biscuit?'

'No thank you.'

'Are you sure? I've got some lovely digestives – I've licked the chocolate off but the biscuity bit's going spare.'

'Erg, thanks, but it's nearly teatime.'

'Is it?' Maude adjusted the elastic on her floppy-brimmed, retro bathing cap and sat back down. 'Hope it tastes better than lunch. That lemon sorbet was as bitter as Cook herself.'

'Anyway,' I continued. 'It's about—'

'Spit it out, child. It's nearly teatime.'

Maude's short-term memory wasn't always the best, though Dad said her forgetfulness was selective. I sat down on the ladybird pouffe beside her and opened the fairy tale book.

'It's about this book – remember it? You used to read it to me at bedtime.'

'Oh yes, I miss our story times,' she said wistfully. 'But I'm not coming back in that castle until your father apologizes to Tyson.'

'So, the book.' I ran my finger over the frayed binding. 'It looks like some of the pages have been torn out.'

'Of course they have. They were about *her*.'

'Her?'

'Yes, *her*.'

'Who's "her"?'

'She's the one we don't talk about; the one they sent away.'

I rubbed my chin. 'If we don't talk about her, why is she in a storybook?'

'Don't be smart with me, missy. Everyone knows we mustn't talk about her.' Aunt Maude glanced over at her eyeball. She licked her lips. 'But woe betide us if we forget her.'

'But who is she?' Maude was obviously getting mixed up again.

'Got marshmallow in your ears, girl? I told you, we don't talk about her. We mustn't talk about her or the place she was sent. Now shush, my eyeball's itching.'

In the jar on the table, the eyeball pulsed.

'Any second now,' said Maude.

Footsteps sounded on the wooden veranda.

'Open the door, will you, child?'

# CHAPTER 8

Emergency. Emergency. I am two minutes late for dinner. I repeat, this is a national emergency. The future of Biscotti is at risk! Or at least you'd think it was, the way Bertie was acting.

'Hurry, Avariella!' he said, folding his arms across his podgy belly and refusing to come inside the caravan. 'You know how Father hates to be kept waiting.'

'Your father needs to get a grip,' Aunt Maude said, appearing in the doorway behind me. 'Now come here and give your old auntie a kiss.'

'I'm afraid I'm too old for that sort of frivolity.' Bertie smoothed down his green velvet knicker-bockers.

'Oh my word, eight years old and already a stuck-up pickle-bottom like your father.'

'Bye, Aunt Maude.' I pulled Bertie away before he had a chance to respond. Pickle-Bottom versus the Toothless Digestive-licker was not a battle I wanted to witness.

Clear of the decking, Bertie wriggled free.

'Aunt Maude is getting worse,' he said, sounding exactly like Dad. 'Pickle-bottom – how vulgar. Have you been there in the caravan with her all day?'

'Not quite.'

'What a shame to miss the celebrations. It was such tremendous fun, Avariella. Dad even allowed me to cut the ribbon when he declared the truffle hog race open.'

*Woopy-doo!* I sometimes wondered if Bertie was really my brother. I couldn't stand all that royal stuff. I nodded and stared up at the castle.

The second sun was sinking behind the Central Tower, sending an orange glow over the smooth stone.

'Oh, and I had an exquisite Viennese marshmallow whirl,' Bertie continued. 'Just the slightest dusting of icing sugar, so it didn't make a mess of my fingers.'

*Viennese whirls – now that was more like it. I hoped we were having something nice for tea . . .*

Whatever we were having, it was being served with a double helping of bad temper. Dad practically exploded when he saw the fairy tale book under my arm.

'Where did you get that?'

'Aunt Maude. She used to read it to me when I was little.'

'What?' Dad's voice was so ridiculously high he sounded like a pixie caught in a mousetrap. 'I thought we'd finally done away with these ridiculous artefacts. Had I known Maude was filling your head with this poppycock, I'd have evicted her from the castle myself.'

'But what if it isn't poppycock?' I said. 'What if the Other World in the story is real? Maude seemed to think—'

'Maude thinks that wretched teabag is alive! I'll hear no more of these ridiculous fairy tales.' Dad waved his hand at the grand piano, nodding in approval as the lid magically lifted and the tinkle of classical music filled the room. 'High culture, this is where your interests should lie. We must not delay your exploration of the finer arts of Biscotti a moment longer.'

Mum yawned. She fiddled with the peacock-feather comb slide in her hair and nodded at Periwinkle. The butler returned her nod, his black toupee slipping forward. He jerked his head back and flicked the hairpiece into place. Coat-tails flapping, he pushed the platinum serving trolley towards the table and lifted the lid on the silver platter. Banoffee burgers. *Yum.*

Dad poked at his burger with his pearl-handled fork. 'Thankfully,' he continued, 'this latest misdemeanour is most timely. Why just today, the Duke of Devilridge advised me of a most excellent governess: Mademoiselle Hornet-Boules—'

'Mademoiselle Hornet-Boules.' Mum pulled a funny face. 'She sounds delightful, dear.'

Dad ignored Mum, drumming his fingers on the polished banqueting table while Periwinkle fetched him a glass of water from the life-sized mermaid fountain.

'The mademoiselle has tutored all the duke's daughters,' he continued. 'But with his youngest, Veronica, now a debutante, she seeks a new position. And what an opportunity. Would you believe she wrote the definitive guide to princess etiquette?'

'Oh, her, *Mrs Expectations.*' Mum stuck her nose in the air and pulled a snooty face.

Even goody-goody Bertie smirked at this.

'This is no joke. As you know, I have always been a fan of the mademoiselle's teaching.'

'As we know indeed, hey, sweetie.' Mum nudged my foot under the table.

'No wonder the children disrespect me, Sophia.' Dad gave Mum the finger wag. His cheeks were so red they were practically sizzling. 'I will take it no more. Good old-fashioned discipline, that's what's needed here.'

Troll poop, this was so not the moment for Doreen and Jeb to burst into the room and give Dad more ammunition. Doreen bleated and charged at the serving trolley, gold-dusted cherries and profiteroles spraying across the carpet. Periwinkle calmly took his white serving gloves off and placed them on the side table. He dug around in the pocket of his black dress trousers and took out a packet of sarsaparilla logs. Doreen's nose twitched. She left the profiterole she was licking and ran at Periwinkle, butting him in the shin.

Periwinkle sighed. 'What have I told you about being gentle, Doreen?' Wiping her muzzle with his tea towel, he picked her up. 'You too, Sir Jeffrey Bobbersons. Come along.'

Dad pushed his plate away. 'Need I say more? This whole household is out of control.'

'Oh, it's just a bit of chocolate, Bertrand.'

'No! It is not just a bit of chocolate. I will hear

no more of this matter. I will be sending for Mademoiselle Hornet-Boules as soon as dinner is over.'

Mum's expression changed. 'But I've already found a new governess – Miss Summer's due to start next week.'

'I am sorry if you have wasted your efforts, but Avariella requires a stricter hand. There are certain—'

'Expectations.' Mum's voice was sad as she completed Dad's sentence, the glance she gave me even sadder. 'Well, be this on your own head, Bertrand, because a caged bird wants nothing more but to fly.'

Too right, Mum. Couldn't have put it better myself. That was it – I was definitely going back to see Ethan and ride on one of those funny bicycles tomorrow. This Hornet-Boules sounded like a complete nightmare. I had to go and take my fun while I still could.

# CHAPTER 9

Ethan didn't seem to recognize me. Maybe it was my PE kit? I didn't know what else to put on, and the purple pleated skirt didn't seem that different from the short skirts I'd seen the girls here wearing. Thinking about it, the pink-and-gold striped vest with the fluffy unicorn on it probably was a bit out there, but what's a princess from another world supposed to do?

Talking of unicorns, that's how I got here. No, not on the back of one, you numpty! By rubbing the unicorn emblem on the fire grate. OK, I admit it, I had to spit on my fingers again to get it to work, but once the emblem was wet it was a straightforward portal transfer back to Camden. And back to Ethan. Now all I needed to do was get his attention. He seemed to be looking everywhere except at me.

'Ethan! Can you hear me?'

Still nothing. I knew I should have brought Jeb, but I was worried he'd wander off when I was on the BMX.

'Ethan. Mr Ethan! It's me – Ava. I've come to have a go on your BMX bike.'

*Finally!* Ethan shrugged and rode slowly over to the gate, pausing to thump fists with one of the wheely-boarders. He must have been riding his BMX really fast because his cheeks were nearly as red as his T-shirt.

'Hi, Ethan,' I said. 'I'm back!'

'So I see.' Ethan smiled and got off his bike.

I waved at the wheely-boarders. They seemed very interested in what we were doing. The girl with her BMX was there too. She was staring at me with her mouth open.

'OK, I did promise.' Ethan nodded towards the far end of the park. 'Let's go over by the play area. You need to learn the rules of the bowl before I take you in there.'

*Rules?* Why did there always have to be rules? I looked over at the wheely-boarders. They were still staring.

'Don't worry,' Ethan said. 'They're all right – just nosy. I think they were meerkats in a former life.' He stood up on his tippy toes with his hands in front of his chest like he was holding a horse's reins and pinched his lips together.

'I'm not worried.'

'Good,' he laughed, 'good.'

OK, between you, me and the witch's gatepost, I had been kind of worried when Ethan didn't come straight over. I thought he might have been ignoring me, that he didn't really think I'd come back. But if he was making jokes about fairy-tale creatures like meerkats, he must want to be my friend. Mustn't he?

Ethan scrunched up his face. 'It wouldn't

hurt to try and blend in a bit, though,' he said apologetically.

I chewed at my fingernails. Being like the other kids is all I've ever wanted, but it's not exactly easy when you're a princess.

'Never mind,' Ethan said. 'You're your own person, sweet. So, do you want to take the bike?'

*Did I!* It was all I'd been thinking about for the last twenty-four hours.

'Ava?'

'Sorry.' I took the bike from Ethan.

'Don't be frightened. Everyone falls off at first – you just have to learn how to fall.'

'Erg, OK.' *Ethan seemed to have me confused with the world's biggest wussy knickers.* 'So how do I start it?'

'Start it? You have ridden a bike before, haven't you?'

I shook my head.

Ethan took off his helmet and ruffled his dirty-blond hair. It was messy and straight and stood up from his head like a bird's nest. 'Here, you best take this. We've got a lot of work to do.'

I reached for the helmet, my hand shaking. I mean, Ethan really needed to work on his coaching technique.

'Right then, Ava. We best start off on the grass. Next time, wear jeans or something so it doesn't hurt as much when you come off.'

Hurt. There he goes again. I mean, Mr Motivation or what . . . And what in the name of the good goblin are jeans?

# CHAPTER 10

Riding a BMX wasn't as easy as I thought. It was a bit like getting on a unicorn – you actually have to learn how to ride the thing. Not that I've ever ridden a unicorn either. Doreen was far too small and Dad would never allow me near a wild one. But anyway, that's not the point. The point is, don't judge me. How was I supposed to know balancing a bike took practice?

'Come on, Ava.' Ethan grabbed hold of the bike seat. 'You're so close. Let's go, one more time.'

'OK.' I smiled – *a princess is not expected to give up when things don't go her way* – but inside I wanted to cry. This was like the zillionth time I'd tried to ride the bike. I was so tired, I'd have slept whether there was a pea under my mattress or not.

'Same as last time,' Ethan said. 'I'll hold the seat, and once you get moving I'll let go.'

I braced myself. My elbow was still throbbing from where I'd fallen off earlier. Ethan said I needed elbow and knee pads, but as we didn't have any I'd just have to try harder not to fall off.

'Ready?'

I nodded.

Ethan grabbed the back of the seat. 'OK. Three. Two. One. *Go!*'

I lifted my foot on to the pedal and pushed down. The bike began to move.

'Pedal,' he shouted, running along behind me. 'Pedal!'

*Like, yay, oh yay with unicorn bells on!* I was doing it. I was riding a BMX bike. Ethan had let go and I was racing along the path. The hairs on

61

my arms rose – I don't know whether it was the breeze or the excitement – but every bit of me felt alive. I turned the handlebars and the bike did exactly what I wanted.

Oh my giddy goblin, this was even better than my potato sack. I picked up speed and zoomed towards the dog-walking area. I felt strong and free. No guilt, no fear, no compromise. Nobody yelling at me, telling me I was rubbish. No *expectations.* Just me and the bike—

*Aaggghh!* A swamp rat ran in front of me and started yapping at my ankles. I pulled back on the brake, but the bike slipped and I fell.

'I think Elvis likes you.' A woman wearing black shiny trousers and a leather jacket scooped up the ratty thing and kissed him on the nose. No wonder he was angry – the only fur on his scrawny grey body was a greased orange quiff. He whimpered and licked the woman's face. He wasn't a rat, after all; he was an Apollonian mountain terrier, although they probably didn't call them that here.

'I hope you didn't hurt him.'

'Hurt him?' What planet was this woman on? I touched my throbbing elbow, blood dripping through my fingers.

'Don't worry, he seems OK,' she continued.

I looked down at the floor. Maybe if I ignored her, she'd get bored and go away . . . oh my giddy goblin, what in the name of the fashion fairy did she have on her feet? The heels on her black boots were so pointy you could use them as skewers.

'Gucci, darling,' she said, seeing me staring. 'I never wear anything else.' She took her sunglasses off and peered down at me. Her disapproving stare looked strangely familiar.

'You OK?' A breathless Ethan offered me his hand.

'Stop fussing, boy,' said the woman. 'She's fine.'

Ethan looked from me to the woman, eyebrows raised. The dog snarled at him, its eyes bulging like it was being strangled. The woman straightened its quiff. Smoothing down her trousers she nudged my foot with her pointy boot.

'A little old to be learning how to ride a bicycle, aren't we?'

I rubbed my goosebumped arms and looked up at the sky. I was totally freezing. The thick black cloud had come from nowhere.

'Are you a late developer? Or perhaps your parents neglect you? That awful outfit would suggest so.'

Growling griffins, was she really still having a pop? So much for ignoring her. Sometimes a

princess had to tackle things head-on.

'*My* awful outfit?' I said, crossing my arms. 'Have you looked in the mirror lately?'

The woman smiled – her teeth as white as the snow-topped peaks of the Apollonian Mountains and perfectly straight. 'Oh, I'm just teasing you, darling,' she said. 'I'm sure Mama and Papa love you in their own way.'

Ethan glared at the woman. She laughed and blew him a kiss. '*Mwah!* Well, I'd love to stay and chat but I have better things to do.' She faked a yawn. 'Like watching paint dry.'

'Off you go then,' Ethan said, waving. 'Don't forget to take your broomstick with you.'

I looked around for a broomstick, but then I remembered there was no magic here. Ethan was insulting her! The woman laughed, a tinkly laugh like unicorn bells. She smoothed down her perfectly straight fringe. Her hair was black and shiny like mine but cut short around her chin.

'A broomstick, now wouldn't that be a marvellous way to avoid the rush hour. What do you think, Avariella?'

'I—'

'Don't answer. I don't have time to waste listening to people answering my questions. Our favourite espresso bar shuts at three. Elvis gets terribly grumpy if he doesn't get his coffee fix.' She held her hand out like she wanted me to shake it but then pulled it away again. 'Mmm, best not. Last time I touched a child I got a terrible rash. Lovely to meet you, darling. I'm sure our cycle paths will cross again.'

# CHAPTER 11

Ethan bent down and picked his bike up, his eyes still on the woman and her ratty dog. 'Who was *that*?'

I shrugged. *How was I supposed to know?*

'Oh, I thought you knew her. She knew your name.'

A shiver ran down my spine like someone had just told me a ghost story. He was right. She did.

'Maybe she heard you say it?' I said.

Ethan didn't look convinced. 'You sure you're OK?'

I wiped the dirt from my elbow. Blood oozed from the graze.

'Come on. Let's go and see Mum.'

Guess what! It turns out Ethan's mum runs the café in the park. Her name is Kaye and she is like so nice – or as Ethan would say, totally chill. Can you believe it? He introduced me to her and I didn't even have to wash my hands and face first!

'And who's this,' she said when we entered the café. 'I've not seen you before. Does your mum know you're hanging about with reprobates like Ethan?'

Ethan rolled his eyes.

'I'm Avariella,' I said. 'I'm very pleased to make your acquaintance.'

'Pleased to meet you too,' Kaye said, pinching her lips together like she was trying not to laugh.

'Ava's not from round here.'

'I see. Sit down, love.'

'Thank you,' I said, trying not to stare at her cropped red hair – lots of women in the Other World had short hair. *What was that all about?*

'Ava's hurt her arm,' Ethan said. 'Can we have the first-aid box.'

'Of course.' Kaye rubbed my shoulder and disappeared behind a tall glass-fronted counter containing a few sad-looking cakes even Doreen would have turned her nose up at. Behind the counter there was a menu board – *Jen's Kitchen*, it said at the top. I wondered who Jen was.

Ethan pulled a metal chair out for me and we sat down. The café wasn't much bigger than the caravan Aunt Maude lived in but it was a lot less interesting. The walls were bare and white, and apart from the menu board, the only decoration was a crinkled poster advertising ice cream.

'There you go.' Kaye put a green plastic box down on the table. 'Where did the sun go?'

Ethan looked out at the rain beating against the window. 'I may as well come home with you then, Mum. Can we have lasagne for tea?' He opened the box and took out a little white packet which he tore open with his teeth. *Like, ow!* Tears pricked my eyes as I wiped my cuts with the stingy little cloth he gave me.

'Sorry, love,' Kaye said. 'But I'm going to be late again – another shift's come up at the pub.'

Ethan rooted in the box and handed me a plaster, trying his best not to look at Kaye.

'I know it's the third night in a row, but with the hoover giving out we really need the money.'

'It's OK,' Ethan said, trying to sound cheerful. 'I've got loads of homework to do anyway.'

Kaye ruffled Ethan's hair. 'Such a good boy.'

'Get off me!' Ethan pushed her hand away but he was smiling.

'How about a milkshake? Heaven knows, young Ava here looks like she needs one.' Kaye walked off towards the counter. Stopping to clear the coffee cups from one of the tables, she stretched out her shoulders and yawned.

Ethan shook his head and turned away.

I wanted to ask him more about his mum and why she had to work so hard, but *a princess is not expected to pry*. Plus, I was pretty sure he didn't want to talk. He'd taken his rectangle out of his pocket and was tapping it with his thumbs. They all seemed to have these strange rectangles here.

I leant over the table, trying to get a better view of it.

Kaye plonked a glass down in front of me. 'You kids and your phones,' she said. 'Don't know how to talk to each other any more.'

I ran my finger down the glass, chasing the dribbles of rich, chocolatey milk that had swooshed over the top. Yumtastic or what! 'Thank you,' I said. 'That really is most generous. Chocolate is my favourite.'

'Ethan's too.' Kaye's warm smile made me strangely sad. 'Such lovely manners,' she said, tucking Ethan's label into his red T-shirt. 'You look out for this one, son. She's special, I can tell.'

'Yes, Mum.' Ethan handed me his phone-rectangle thingy. 'Hey, Ava, check this flair out.'

*Like, no way*, there were moving pictures of a man on a BMX doing a backflip. It was like looking into a crystal gazer only the images were clearer. No wonder people were always staring at these things.

'Who is he?'

'Rad Tyreless, X-Games Big Air gold medal

winner for the last three years.'

'Can you do that on your BMX?'

Ethan laughed. 'I wish.' He took a slurp of milkshake, swooshing the straw around his glass to make the milk froth. 'I'm more into racing really... or at least I used to be.'

'Used to be?'

'Yes, when Dad was here to take me to the meets.'

I sipped my drink. The froth had disappeared and the surface was flat and murky. Should I ask Ethan about his dad? It seemed like something a friend would do, but I wasn't sure and he was already looking at his phone again. He scrolled through the pictures of people riding BMX.

'I've been thinking of starting again,' he said without looking up from the screen. 'I mean, dude, I'm old enough to take myself to meets now, aren't I?'

'Yes,' I said, even though I wasn't sure if that was the right answer. 'So why don't you.'

A chair scraped on the tiled floor. There was a man at the table next to us with a small child. He took the boy's coat off and gave him a book to look at.

Ethan stared at the man wistfully. He leant back in his chair and sighed. 'How about you?' he said, looking at my elbow. 'Still want to ride BMX?'

# CHAPTER 12

*S till want to ride BMX?*

*Do I!* I mean, riding a bike is the best thing ever. I'd never felt so free. And I actually think I could be good at BMX. Ethan thought so too. He said, next time I came to the park he'd show me some tricks. Which is like brill – better than brill even. Except he also said I should wear *proper clothes*, something that covered my knees and arms.

And he was right. It wasn't just the getting hurt – I needed to blend in more. I didn't want people asking any more questions. People like that rude woman in the funny boots. I'd seen her again when I was walking back along the river. Would you believe, her dog did a poo and she didn't even pick it up?

'Ava, are we playing chess or not?' Bertie poked his head round the door of his walk-in closet.

'I suppose, if we have to.'

I screwed up Bertie's fencing tights and threw them on the floor below the endless rails of knickerbockers. I'd tried them on because they were the closest thing to those stretchy Other World trousers I could think of, but they were far too small and forest-green really wasn't my colour.

Bertie tutted. 'Of course, we don't *have to*. But if anyone should master this fine art, it's you. Chess is a most excellent tool for teaching sustained concentration and perseverance.'

*What is it with my brother? He's eight and he talks like a professor.*

Bertie threw his leg over his tortoise-stool and

sat down on the cushion fitted into the recess of its shell. The tortoise poked its head out and waddled over to the felt-topped games table in the bay window. I'd been so jealous when Mum gave Bertie the giant tortoise – a walking seat and a pet combined in one, what's not to like? But then Mum had brought in *my* present – Jeb – and I forgot all about wanting a tortoise-seat.

Bertie straightened his gleaming chessboard – he'd obviously been polishing it again. 'What's with the sudden interest in fencing anyway?' He looked at my arm. 'My goodness, are you being bullied? Was it Simone?'

Simone is Cook's granddaughter. She helps out in the kitchen sometimes. We used to play together until Dad suddenly decided we weren't allowed to any more. Now whenever Simone sees me, she pulls a face like a baboon sucking a lemon.

I shrugged and sat down opposite Bertie, staring at the rain. Jeb jumped down off the bed and curled up at my feet. I tickled him with my toes. What was with the weather? It hardly ever rained in Biscotti, but this afternoon the sky had been heavy with billowing black clouds that shifted and churned like candyfloss in the confectioner's machine. It was almost like the storm had followed me back from Camden.

'See,' Bertie said. 'I told you the sky must burst at some point. Science dictates it.'

I nodded. Yep, it had burst all right. Big-style. Just before tea when I was playing down at the moat with Jeb. Periwinkle had gone ballistic when we trampled mud into the hall. He's someone else who will never join my fan club. Oh well, at least I have Jeb . . . and chocolate.

I rubbed the rim of my magic pot. 'Lime,' I said, tapping the spoon against the copper surface three times.

The bottom of the pot filled with a rich, citrus-scented liquid. There was a bang and a cloud of steam rose into the air, leaving behind a perfect lime truffle.

'Heaven,' said Bertie, grabbing the truffle and biting into the crispy chocolate shell.

I tutted and made another. It was a good job

the enchanted pot only worked for its owner or my brother would be the size of a prize hog.

'Make your move then.' Bertie pointed a chocolatey finger at the chessboard.

'Actually, I'm really tired. I think I'm going to have an early night.'

Bertie's lip curled downwards. 'But you never go to bed early.'

I stared at the map of the seven realms on his wall. I felt bad not playing with Bertie, but for once I needed to be alone. My head was so full of bikes and the strange world I'd visited, I didn't have room for anything else. Especially something double boring like chess.

Bertie leant across the table. 'Are you sure you're not being bullied? By Jove, I'll set the knights on her.'

'Nobody is bullying me, Bertie,' I said, standing up and walking past the bookshelf packed with leather-bound encyclopedias and study guides. I couldn't tell him the truth. He was such a goody-goody, he was bound to snitch on me.

'Goodnight then.' Bertie pretended to concentrate on putting the chess set away, but I could see him watching me under his curly fringe.

It wasn't really his fault, the way he acted. He spent too much time with Dad. There were *certain expectations* for Bertie too. He was just better at meeting them.

'Goodnight,' I said, turning the door handle. 'Maybe we can play chess tomorrow.'

# CHAPTER 13

I switched the hanger on the door knob to 'Princess Sleeping' and shut my bedroom door behind me. *Think, Ava. Think.* There must be some way to get the things I needed to ride the BMX again. There had to be. I put the magic chocolate pot on the bed and, almost tripping over Jeb, who was lying on the rug gnawing his dragon-claw chew, pulled my fairy tale book from the shelf. I flicked to the story about the Land Magic Forgot and stared at the picture of the high street.

All those shops. Maybe I could trade something to get the things I needed? My magic pot must be worth loads more than those funny trousers. I picked up the little pot and polished it on my sleeve, doubt fizzing in my throat. It was a christening present from Zana, my godmother. That and the ring . . .

The ring! That was it. I rummaged under my bed for my ballerina jewellery box. Maybe I didn't have to say goodbye to the pot after all. I lifted the lacquer lid and the tiny ballerina sprang to life. She stretched and began to perform a dance in time with the tinkly music. I've always felt sorry for the boxed ballerina-fairy.

I wanted to release her but Dad said we couldn't interfere with fairy law and she had to earn her freedom.

'Fetch the wish ring please, ballerina.'

There was a flash of light and the ballerina lifted the ring up above her head like a strongman lifting a dumbbell.

'There you go, duck,' she said in a voice that belonged more to a seven-foot mountain troll than to a tiny fairy. 'Now do you remember how to use it?'

I nodded, but the ballerina continued to tell me anyway. Then she laid into all the reasons why my wish probably wouldn't be granted. I shut my jewellery box. She knocked angrily on the lid but eventually went back to sleep.

I held the ring up to the brass oil lamp. Light danced from the turquoise crystal like it was alive. Of course I remembered how to use it. I'd been building up to this all my life. But I'd never had a wish the Fairy Council were likely to consider worthy before. You probably don't want to hear this, but the whole three-wish thing –

well, it works differently in real life. You can't just wish for anything. I mean, this is Biscotti – my dad's in charge – wishes aren't supposed to be fun. Oh no, there are rules and regulations which are monitored by the Fairy Council. Rule number 167893 states: *a wish will only be granted if it's pure, sustainable and comes from the heart.*

Yes, I know, gobbledegook. I have no idea what that means either. Nobody does. This is why the wish granters have wishometers. Don't ask me how they work – if I understood magic I'd wish up my own BMX gear. But I did know that if I wanted my godmother to grant my wish, I would have to set her wishometer off.

I slipped the ring on my finger. Closing my eyes, I rubbed the crystal and wished: *please give me the things I need to blend in and ride BMX in the Other World.*

Nothing.

I squeezed my eyelids together and wished again. I kept them closed for ages, waiting for the flash of light, the coloured smoke or Zana's husky voice.

Still nothing.

That familiar empty feeling rose up from the pit of my stomach. I touched the graze on my elbow and thought of all the reasons why I needed to ride that bike. How it made me feel, free and light like a dragon flying high above the Apollonian Mountains. And how I needed to see Ethan. To have a friend all of my own. A proper friend who actually thought I might be good at something for once.

And Ethan needed a friend too. I just knew it.

I wished again.

# CHAPTER 14

They say be careful *what* you wish for, but nobody warns you to be careful *who* you wish for. Trust me, they should. This was not exactly a dream-come-true kind of moment. I'd almost given up on the wish when the candelabra above my bed shook and something silver thudded to the floor. It looked like a giant turkey wrapped in tinfoil. Jeb jumped up from the rug, the fur on his neck rising. He barked at the turkey which was now spinning like a manic tornado.

When the spinning eventually stopped, I could see the turkey was actually a man. An extremely tall man wearing a silver jumpsuit with a lime-green fur collar. His army boots pounding on the wooden floor, he walked over and flashed his identity badge at me: Officer of the Fairy Council.

'Oh, it's you!' he said, scratching his stubbly chin. 'Zana warned me you might be an early developer.' He poked me with his moon-topped wand. '*Spirited*, she said. You don't look spirited to me. You look like a maggot.'

'I beg your pardon—'

'Whatever. Now shut that furball up and let's get this over with. As if I 'aven't 'ad enough to deal with today, what with folks getting spooked by the storm left right and centre.'

I picked Jeb up. *Like, who was this awful man?*

'Late for me tea, I was.' He took a notebook the size of an encyclopedia out of his pocket. 'Missus had grilled some lovely squirrel too.'

'Like, who even are—'

'Don't turn yer nose up at me, Maggot. We

can't all eat swan and live in a castle.'

'You're frightfully rude,' I said, trying to sound royal and commanding. 'And I would never eat swan. Now where's Zana?'

'Retired. Her bunions kept playing up. Her and her sisters packed it in at the same time, lazy old hags. Gone to a retirement home in another realm. Good riddance, I say. I'm in charge of yer wishes now. The name's Nigel, but you can call me the Godfather.'

The Godfather swatted a fly away from his bald head. He had ears like the pitta breads I'd seen in Kaye's café. They were huge.

'Right, name.'

'Avariella Petulia Winifred Pandoro D'Allessandro of Biscotti.'

The Godfather sniggered. 'Yes, 'ere you are.'

His book flicked open to a page with my picture on it. The pale blue marks on the page grew darker to reveal a load of swirly writing.

'Ooh, I don't like this one bit. Says here I'm to give you a BMX, appropriate clothing and safety gear and whatever else you need to go off and play hooky with your mate in the Other World.' He shook his wrist. The thick strap on his wishometer was made out of the same lime-green fur as his collar. 'Must be something wrong with me gauge,' he said, tapping the glass. He looked at me like I'd just stolen his last chocolate. 'Oh, this is way beyond my pay scale.'

Mumbling to himself, the Godfather took a tiny blue crystal ball out of his pocket and rubbed it. Holding the crystal in his palm, he began to speak. A squeaky voice spoke back. Unfortunately, they were talking Aorphnian, the language of the magically gifted, so I couldn't understand them. I twisted my fingers through Jeb's fur, trying not to stare at the Godfather's ears.

'Right,' he said, placing the crystal back in his pocket. 'Me mate Bob agrees, I'm not paid enough to be landed with this sort of responsibility.'

He rummaged around in his pocket again and took out an ink pad and rubber stamp. Opening his giant, leather-bound notebook, he stamped the page with my picture on it and tore out the one below. He rolled up the thick yellowy parchment and tapped me on the head with it before handing it to me.

'Wish denied?' I said. 'What do you mean, wish denied?'

'What do you think it means, genius?'

'But I triggered your wishometer.'

'Don't you wishometer me. That may be but you've also set off me queenie-will-kill-me bell.'

'There's no such thing.'

He pointed at his chest and it began to glow. A badge appeared in the shape of the royal shield. 'By royal order, this badge says. Your mam put in a special request for me to take over as the royal advisor when Zana jacked it in. Very grateful to her I am. So if something's likely to upset our queenie, then it's a no.'

*What?* He had to be lying. Mum putting in a special request for this idiot?

'But you have to grant my wish. The constitution says so.'

'Look, appeal to the Council if you will. But, I'm telling yer, they're not daft enough to get on the wrong side of Old King Frilly Knickers. Not after the Great Banishment.'

'Banishment?'

'Oops, me and me big gob. I forgot, nobody's meant to talk about that.' He tapped his bulbous nose. 'Likes to keep his skeletons in his cupboard, yer dad.'

I thought about what Aunt Maude had said: *we mustn't talk about her or the place she was sent.* 'What kind of skeletons exactly?' I said.

The Godfather yawned. 'Right, I'm off—'

There was a puff of green smoke. The Godfather did a little jig like he had ants in his pants and pulled out his crystal gazer.

'What now?' he said, placing the crystal in the flat of his hand.

This time the squeaky voice belonged to a woman – and she was speaking Biscottian.

'Hold on.' The Godfather stepped into my closet. 'Private,' he said, slamming the door.

I pressed my ear against the polished wood but he must have gone right to the back because all I could hear was muffled squeaks. I put Jeb down on the floor and gave him his dinosaur claw. Chewing my hair, I waited for the Godfather.

'Right, change of plan,' he said, finally emerging from the closet. 'It looks like you get yer wish. Now stand back.'

*What had changed?* Was that Zana on the crystal gazer?

The Godfather waved his wand and the room filled with green smoke. 'Bad idea if you ask me – which nobody ever does.'

When the smoke eventually cleared, the Godfather was standing next to a beautiful lilac BMX. *Like, wow! Wow! Wow!* I ran towards the bike. It was so totally cool.

'Safety first.' The Godfather stepped in front of the BMX and handed me a silver bike pump.

I ran my finger over the emblem on the pump: a raised letter P.

'Be careful with that, and keep it with yer at all times. You never know when yer might need it.'

*Erg, like OK.* He was talking nonsense again. I leant to the side trying to get a proper look at my BMX and the Other World clothes that were hanging over it. There was a rucksack too, with a matching wallet and a helmet and water bottle.

'Now the rules: first off, do not breathe a word of Biscotti to anyone.'

*As if. After the way Ethan had reacted to my princess dress, you didn't need to be a genius to work out that was a bad idea.*

'I mean it.' The Godfather tapped his wand across his hand. 'One word and I'll turn you and that fluffball to dragon dung.'

*That sounds painful. Point noted.*

'They'll just think yer away with the fairies, anyway,' he continued, giving Jeb a look that made him whimper. 'Or worse still, a baby. You don't want people thinkin' yer a baby now, do yer?'

*Blah blah blah . . . just give me the bike.*

'Are you listening? Because this is important – following the correct portal protocol is paramount.' The Godfather pointed his finger at me and started to spout some daft nursery rhyme:

'It starts with a kick,

'A kick of the heel,

'With a bit of spit, it opens no big deal,
'But do make sure to secure it again,
'By tapping twice and counting to ten.'
Oh, my giddy goblin, this man was a lunatic.
'Got it?' he said.
'Got it,' I repeated. *Like, whatever it takes for you to give me the BMX!*

# CHAPTER 15

Oh my curly candy, I just love riding BMX. Apart from sack-racing, it's the only thing I've ever been any good at. Or at least I *thought* I was good at it when we were practising tricks on the flat concrete behind the children's play area. I could do endos, no problem, and bunny hops and bar spins. I could even do a tail whip – Ethan said it took him ages to get the knack of that move. But I couldn't get my head around the bowl.

That's what they call the grey crater thing

where I first saw Cleo on her BMX. Ethan was trying to teach me to air out of it – to fly into the air and twist my bike around – but it just wasn't happening.

'Go on, Ava.' Ethan touched my arm. 'What are you waiting for?' he said. 'You're well ready for this.'

What was I waiting for? Erg, I wasn't quite sure, but if everyone could just stop staring at me that might help. My new friends, the wheely-boarders Ant and Kai, peered eagerly over from the other side of the bowl and Cleo was watching my every move.

'Remember,' she said, 'stay loose on the bike.'

I nodded and tightened my helmet. Checking the opposite corner of the bowl was clear, I dropped into the concrete basin, keeping the bike at an angle. Eyes on the opposite ramp, I pedalled forward.

'Go on, Ava,' called Ethan.

I wanted to make him happy, I so did. But each time I went to jump, I froze. I couldn't do it – no matter how hard I tried.

I slowed and let my bike slide backwards into the bowl.

'No big deal,' Ant called from the top of the bowl. 'Cleo forgets not everyone gets it straight away.'

Cleo and Ant are twins. They have this spooky thing going on where they know what each other is thinking. It's like totally weird because even though they think the same, apart from their dark, curly hair they look nothing alike. Cleo is small and sparrow-like while Ant is more a cross between a giraffe and a rhino.

I smiled but I didn't feel happy. Up until now I had got everything straight away. What was wrong with me? I'd been trying all day and I was actually worse than when I started.

'One more time?'

I shook my head at Ethan. I'd been riding so much my legs were wobbling. I'd try again next weekend. I pushed my bike up out of the bowl.

'You'll get it,' Cleo said, pulling at a thread on her denim cut-offs. 'You just need to practise more. You should come to BMX camp with me.

We can bunk together.'

Ethan shook his head. 'Not everyone has parents who poop money, you know.'

'Harsh, dude.' Kai picked up his skateboard and hugged it to his chest.

A *skateboard* is the proper name for those wheely-board things I told you about. And talking of proper names, Kai is the proper name for Ollie, the boy with the shorts and straight hair. Who it turns out isn't called Ollie at all. Rather, an ollie is the name of a skateboard trick. The Other World is so confusing.

'Sorry.' Ethan gave Cleo an unsure smile. He knew she was really looking forward to her week-long BMX camp in the school holidays.

'No worries.' Cleo tapped her orange-painted fingernail against her teeth. 'You OK, Ethy?'

'Just a bit tired. Late night again. Mum was working at the pub and I was worried about her coming home in the dark after the trouble on the estate.'

Cleo looked at Ant. He nodded. 'Hey, you guys want to come for pizza with us?' he said.

Cleo linked arms with me. Like actually linked arms with me. Dancing unicorns, nobody apart from my family had ever done that before. 'Please come,' she said. 'It'll be fun.'

'What do you say, Ava?' Ethan rummaged in his jeans pocket. He bent down to pick up a gold coin he'd dropped. 'You hungry?'

Hungry? I was starvanche, but I had no idea if the paper money the Godfather had left me would be enough to pay for this pizza food. In Biscotti, I wasn't allowed to carry money.

'I'll shout you a slice,' said Cleo, as though reading my mind.

'I couldn't possibly—'

'Come on. That's what friends are for . . .'

I felt all warm inside, like I'd just eaten a bowl of apple pie and custard. Cleo thought of me as her friend. This was turning into the best day since Mum had given me Jeb. I just hoped I liked pizza.

# CHAPTER 16

**O**h my growling griffin, pizza is like the best thing ever! Well, maybe it's not as good as BMX but it's up there with chocolate fountains and ice cream sundaes. Cleo and Ant led the way to this little café that smelt of hot cheese. We had to queue up in front of a glass counter and point at the pizza slice we wanted. Then a shiny-faced man in a shiny red apron put it on a tray and asked if we'd like a drink. I had a slice of pepperoni and a Coke because that's what Ethan had.

We sat in a booth in the window, Kai, Cleo and Ant squashing together on one seat and me and Ethan sitting opposite.

'So,' Cleo said. 'Ryan wants to know when you're coming back to training.'

Ethan ignored Cleo. 'Not eating your pizza,' he said, nudging my tray.

I poked at the pizza. Everyone was eating with their fingers, but it was loaded with herby tomato sauce which made it all floppy and I wasn't sure what to do. *A princess is not expected to get food on her fingers when dining.* Cleo smiled and pulled off some of the gooey cheese oozing from her slice of ham and mozzarella. She squashed it into a ball and popped it on the end of her tongue. I glanced sideways down the restaurant and did the same.

*Yumtastic or what?* I grabbed the pizza slice and took a humongous bite.

'Ethan?' Cleo brushed a crumb off Ant's red-and-black lumberjack shirt. He huffed and pushed her hand away. 'There's this big coach visiting from the US,' she continued. 'Ryan said

100

he'll be working with the junior racing club.'

'Who's Ryan?' I asked, wiping tomato sauce from my chin.

'Ethan's coach,' said Ant. 'Or at least he used to be.'

Ethan pushed his tray away. His cheeks were bright red. He stared out of the window while the rest of us finished our pizza in silence. 'Look, Ava,' he said, slurping down the last of his Coke. 'Isn't that the weird woman from the park?'

'Yes. Yes, it is.'

Her hair was different – it was cut into a sort of bowl shape and dyed kingfisher blue – but it was definitely her. Her dog saw us through the window and barked – his quiff had been dyed blue too.

'Hey, that's the lady who was asking about Ava last week,' Kai said. 'Odette.'

'What?' I sat up straight.

The woman called Odette yanked the dog's lead and pulled him away from the window. She didn't look at us, even though Elvis was going off on one big-style.

'She wanted to know where you were from.'
Kai scrunched up his face. 'Where *do* you live?'

I shuffled in my seat. 'The other side of the lock,' I said. Which was sort of true.

'Check out her Perspex wedges.' Cleo leant closer to the window. 'Radical or what.'

Ethan shrugged. 'Radical? She's totally creepy. Why would she want to know where Ava lives?'

The pizza churned in my stomach. Yes, *why*? There was something about this woman that just didn't feel right. She was on the other side of the street now, near the bike stand where we'd left our BMXs. Leaning against a shiny black car, she held her rectangle phone to her ear, waving her free hand about like she was conducting an orchestra.

Ethan's phone beeped. He stared at the screen. 'I have to go. Mum's short on milk at the café. Ready, Ava?'

'Sure.' My bike was locked up with Ethan's. I was glad. I didn't want to have to walk past that scary Odette woman by myself.

Seeing us cross the road, she stopped talking

and put her phone in her oversized handbag. 'Avariella,' she said. 'I'm charmed.'

'Why have you been asking about Ava?' Ethan said, holding his bike helmet in front of him.

Odette's dark blue eyes widened. Her black eyeliner was finished with a neat flick at the outer edge of each lid. 'And good day to you too, young man,' she said.

'Whatever.' Ethan went to unlock the bikes.

'My friends said you were looking for me,' I said apologetically. That was a bit rude of Ethan.

'Not me, darling. Elvis.'

'Your dog was looking for me?' He was barking at the cars and hadn't even noticed I was there.

'Yes. For some unfathomable reason he seems to have taken a liking to you.'

I glanced over to the pizza-shop window where Cleo was peering at me anxiously.

Odette smiled – or maybe it was a grimace – either way it wasn't exactly friendly. 'No matter. I'll not be requiring your services now anyway.'

'My services?'

'Yes, Elvis was hoping you could help out with a bit of dog-minding while I was away perusing a little off-shore development.'

I screwed up my face – why would she ask a stranger to dog sit?

'But I'm afraid you've missed out on the opportunity to serve me.'

*The opportunity to serve her? Like, woe is me.*

'I've taken the plunge and signed the contract. I was literally just sorting the final details. I've decided to supervise the early stages of the project myself.'

'That's nice,' I said.

'Delightful. I thought there might have been a few more barriers to my relocation. I mean, it's not everyone's cup of tea – a theme park – but it turns out the doors were wide open.'

Odette's smile made the hairs on my neck stand up.

'I just hope the weather settles down again. There was a terrible storm on my last visit.'

*What was it with these Other World folk and the weather?*

'Anyway, I wanted to wish you good luck.'

'Good luck?'

'Come on, Ava.' Ethan handed me my BMX.

When I turned round again, Odette was gone.

# CHAPTER 17

Oh my giddy goblin, Mademoiselle Hornet-Boules is the worst. She'd only been my governess for a few weeks but it already felt like a lifetime. At this rate I might just lock myself in a dingy tower – and throw away the key.

'Faster, girl!' The mademoiselle tapped her cane across her hand. 'You should be able to balance a blancmange on your head by now. What is wrong with you?'

*What's wrong with me? Like, hello!* I lifted my

hands ready to catch the silver serving plate, and picked up pace.

'*Non. Non. Non.*' Mademoiselle Hornet-Boules's skirt made a swishing sound as she crossed the room. She jerked my hand away and peered over the top of her half-moon glasses. 'No cheating. Now try again.'

*Think of BMX. Think of BMX. Think of BMX. Think of Ethan and your friends.*

Yes, friends.

I had friends! And I'd been having such a brilliant time in the Other World with them.

'Concentrate, girl.' Mademoiselle Hornet-Boules poked me with her cane. 'Back straight. See how I hold mine.'

Everything about Mademoiselle Hornet-Boules was straight. Her back. Her nose. Her thin pencilled eyebrows. Even the black ribbon she tied around the tight bun that sat in the exact centre of her head. *Symmetry is important,* mon enfant. *It keeps society on the right track. You must not stray from the path that has been allocated to you.*

The path that has been allocated to me? Like, why did being the heir to the throne mean I wasn't allowed to be me? I didn't even want to be Queen. I wanted to eat pizza and win a gold medal in the Olympics. I took another step forward. The tray thundered to the floor, the blancmange narrowly missing Hornet-Boules's buckled patent leather shoe.

'Leave it, child,' she said. 'My nerves will not take any more of you.' She adjusted her glasses. 'Now quickly. The royal carriage leaves in five minutes.'

Today I was going with my family to unveil a new statue of Dad at the harbour in Bourbon. On the plus side, I got out of my lesson in *domestic accounting*, but the downside was having to sit in a carriage with Dad for two hours. I ran down the back stairs and through the servants' quarters to fetch Jeb. He was in the herb garden with Doreen, his unicorn onesie streaked with dirt. Mum had bought the onesie especially because the argento unicorns had been sighted near Silver-Oak River. She promised we could go and see them on the way to Bourbon.

'Chickens have all scarpered,' Cook said, shaking her head at Doreen and Jeb who were now whizzing around the vegetable cart. She wiped a bead of sweat from her forehead with her frilled apron and put her hands on her hips, her round face as red as a sugar dummy. 'Tell your father, if there's no eggs for breakfast in the morning it's your fault.'

'My fault!'

'Yours and that daft-looking dog. Poor chickens don't get a moment's peace with him.' Cook disliked Jeb even more than she disliked me. 'Not my place to say it, I know.'

*But you're going to.*

'But this family's cursed with wayward women ...'

'Yes, Cook,' I said, racing off across the patio.

Doreen bleated excitedly and started to follow.

'Sorry, Do-Do. There's no chance Dad will let you come. Not after you ate the speech he'd prepared.'

The tiny unicorn looked sad for a moment but then she noticed a turnip that had fallen off the vegetable cart. She nudged it with her nose and started to munch it.

As usual, I was last in the carriage. Bertie rolled his eyes at Mum and Dad who were arguing in hushed voices about some blue stone and the weather. I pulled Jeb's hood over his ears and turned towards the window. It wasn't far to Silver-Oak River. Even Mum and Dad couldn't argue when the magnificent argento unicorns were about.

But the unicorns weren't about. There was plenty of their rainbow glitter poop along the grassy riverbank but not a single unicorn.

'I don't understand,' said Bertie, waving his notebook. 'Their seasonal visit usually lasts at least two weeks. I've been recording it here in my natural history log since I was three years old. They don't leave until they've eaten all the silver acorns. It's the acorns that give their manes the silver hue.'

'It is odd,' Mum said, winding the carriage window down. 'Very odd.' She poked her head out of the window. 'Pull over, please,' she shouted to the coachman.

The coach trundled to a stop under the shade of a giant silvern-oak. I followed Mum out of the carriage, the acorns crunching under my feet. Jeb woofed. The knitted horn on his unicorn onesie bobbing from side to side, he ran in and out of the silver-grey trees. Mum smiled. But then she picked up one of the glittery silver acorns that were the favourite food of the unicorns and her expression changed.

'Perfect,' she said, pressing the acorn between her fingers and holding it up to the light. 'Something must have startled them.'

'Like what?' I asked.

'I don't know, pumpkin. But it takes a lot to startle a unicorn. As for scaring them enough to move on altogether before they've eaten all the acorns – that's unheard of.'

'Unheard of?' I lifted up the hem of my frilly, satin dress and climbed awkwardly into the carriage, Jeb pushing past me to get the best seat. *What I wouldn't do for a pair of jeans.*

'Stop putting ideas into their heads,' Dad said, folding up his copy of the *Biscotti Herald*. 'I'm sure it's nothing.'

'I wouldn't be so sure,' said Mum. She picked up Dad's paper and flicked through the pages, stopping at a full-page picture of a cactus-like plant covered in small black flowers.

'Wart blossom,' Bertie gasped. 'It grows in twenty-year cycles. It's not due to flower for another two years.'

Dad tutted and folded up the paper, the pages catching in the breeze as the coachman set off again. 'Nature is not a science,' he said. 'No doubt, all that rain we had brought it on.'

'It's used for dark magic,' Bertie said.

'And for good.' Dad did a sort of sideways karate chop which meant the conversation was over.

I sank back into the soft velvet cushions and closed my eyes. I'd already done a full day on my BMX in Camden this morning. A double life was fun but hard work.

'Those awful trolls.' Mum coughed and wound up the window. She picked up Dad's paper and wafted it in front of her nose, trying to get rid of the eggy pong coming from Swamp Diavolo, the flat marshland on the edge of Bourbon. She fingered the turquoise crystal she wore constantly around her neck. 'But about the wart blossom,' she said. 'It wouldn't hurt to ask the Godfather—'

There was a flash of green light.

Dad cried out as the Godfather thudded through the roof of the carriage and landed sideways across his knee.

'Someone say me name?'

Dad pushed the Godfather on to the floor. Barking excitedly, Jeb jumped from my knee and lay down on Nigel's chest, snarling.

'Behave, fluffball.' The Godfather batted Jeb away. He dusted down his silver jumpsuit and crouched on one knee in front of Mum like he was about to propose. 'Now what can I do for yer, Queenie.'

Mum opened the paper. 'What do you make of this?'

'Wart blossom – very good for sweaty armpits.'

Dad and Bertie stuck up their noses in unison.

'You don't think the fact it's appearing all over the kingdom is strange?'

'Bumper year. I know I'll be stocking up. Sick of the missus smelling like death himself.'

Mum sighed. 'But Nigel, it's not due to flower for another two years? And what with the storm, and the unicorns disappearing.'

Nigel shrugged. 'Coincidence, ma'am. That's all. You don't want to be reading owt into what those stuck-up 'orses with 'orns do – can't trust a unicorn as far as you can throw it.'

'But they've fed here since Biscotti began,' Bertie said, taking his logbook out of his satchel.

'Time they 'ad a change then, innit.' Nigel drummed his fingers on the floor. 'Now will that be all? Only I'm due to clock off in five minutes. It's toad-racing night down the club.'

Mum stared at me intently. I stared back. 'Are you sure there's not something going on?' she said.

'Listen to the man,' Dad said. 'What's the point calling him here if you don't listen?'

The Godfather puffed his chest out importantly. 'Too right, sire. Trust me. If there was anything going on, I'd know.'

# CHAPTER 18

Oh yay, oh yay with unicorn bells on, like how cool. Ethan has finally decided to race again. And you won't believe it, but he's brought me along to Leanne Valley to watch his training session. Awesome, or what? My eyes nearly popped out my head when I saw the track, twisting and coiling like a dusty beige snake around the stadium. It has this massive start hill – it's so big it's practically a mountain. That's where Ethan is now, lined up with the other riders...

Troll poop – I covered my eyes with my hands

– Ethan was last out the gate again. But by the good goblin, he soon caught up. He chased the other riders down the hill and into the long straight rhythm section, catching them on the berm, where he zoomed into first place. Like wow, he was fast: faster than a witch trying to get to the magic store sales.

I wandered over to him but the coach got there first. 'Nice!' He held his hand out and they thumped fists. 'Bro, you have real talent. But you need to get your head around the gate.'

Ethan nodded.

'You're thinking too much. Buzzer, barrier, *go*!' He patted Ethan on the shoulder and headed back towards the changing rooms.

I smiled at Ethan but he wouldn't even look at me.

'Are you, OK?' I said. 'Maybe the coach-man is right.'

'What would you know? You've never even been in the gates. *Coach-man* – go back to your princess dress, why don't you.'

'Ethan—' My throat tightened like I'd

swallowed a piece of poisoned apple.

'Go on then. Off you go. I knew I shouldn't have brought you here.'

My cheeks burnt. Why was he taking it out on me? Go back to my princess dress?

Growling griffins, I'd show him.

Standing up on the start hill was like being on top of the world. Not because I could see lots, but because of the way it made me feel – brave and strong and daring like a knight about to go into battle. I may not have been in the gates before but I'd done enough sack-sledging to know something about take-offs.

I released the brake and went for it.

Blood thundered in my ears as I hurtled down the ramp, the pedals turning so fast my foot slipped. But no way was I going to brake. I hit the bottom and, finding my pedal again, sped towards the triple jump where I took the first hump and flew smoothly into the air, landing without even a wobble. *Sick.* I looked back over my shoulder to see if Ethan had noticed but I couldn't see him. Instead, in the exact spot where he'd been standing was that creepy Odette woman from the park. And she was looking right at me.

My bike teetered like a one-legged dog. I tuned back into the track and straightened the handlebars. When I glanced towards the woman again, she was holding hands with a small child. What was wrong with me?! It wasn't Odette at all. Ever since Kai had told me about her looking for me in the park, I'd been totally paranoid.

I quickened my pace, ready to take the jump. But it was too late. I'd lost too much speed. My bike slipped and I toppled sideways, landing on my hip. There was a screech followed by a thud and a wheel hit me in the back. Someone shouted *stop*!

'Sorry,' I cried to the rider who had fallen from her bike beside me. 'Sorry.'

'Hey, no probs.' She stood up and offered me her hand. 'But you should probably stick to the beginners' sessions.'

*How embarrassing!* If I'd ever wanted a griffin

to swoop down and swallow me it was now.

I felt a hand on my shoulder. 'It's OK, Ava.' Ethan picked my bike up. 'Come on.'

I hesitated for a moment, but the other BMXers were growing impatient. I took a deep breath and followed him over to the red plastic seats in the spectator area. He leant my bike against the barrier and sat down, tapping the space next to him.

'I'm sorry, Ava.'

I shrugged. Saying sorry didn't make the mean things Ethan had said go away.

'It's just the last time I raced here, I was with Dad.'

That was the first time I'd ever heard him talk about his dad.

'It's OK,' I said. 'That must be hard.'

Ethan nodded. He stared down at the floor. I waited for him to tell me more but he didn't, and *a princess is not expected to pursue an issue when others wish the matter closed.* What could I do to make him feel happy again? Nothing, really, but I could buy him pizza.

# CHAPTER 19

I wasn't sure if it was the breeze that made me shiver or the buildings. There were three of them, flat-fronted towers the colour of waffle cones, reaching up to touch the sky. Ethan lived in the middle one. Its windows shone like cats' eyes in moonlight, stealing the light. We climbed off our bikes and wheeled them through the entrance and towards the lifts.

The lift was like totally freaky. It just wasn't natural to travel in a tiny silver box like that. I squeezed my eyelids tightly together refusing to open them until we shuddered to a stop on the twenty-first floor. Ethan gave me a few seconds to get it together, then led me along a narrow corridor lined with brown doors. At the end of the corridor he stopped. The fluorescent light above our head flickered and went out.

'Great, just what we need, Mum coming home late down an unlit corridor. Now bring your bike in or it will get nicked.'

I pushed my bike into the magnolia hall.

'Are you cold?' Ethan asked, seeing me rub my goosebumped arms.

'I'm fine.' It wasn't that cold and I had my hoodie if I needed it.

'This is why I don't have friends round.'

'Don't be silly. It's very homely.'

Ethan rolled his eyes so far back they looked like ping-pong balls. 'It's a dump. Sit down, I'll go and get us a drink.'

I sat down on the battered sofa. Kaye had covered it with a colourful patchwork throw but that didn't help disguise the broken springs. I shimmied along to the next seat. Even worse – as well as the springs I could feel a bump. I put my hand under the cushion and pulled out a pea. It was rock-hard and the colour of dried snot. I put it on the table.

My bum wasn't the only part of me that felt uncomfortable. I don't want to be rude about Ethan's home, but it felt sort of sad. Everything was really old, and even though it was full of ornaments and photographs, somehow it seemed empty. I wandered towards the floor-length window, stopping in front of the fireplace to look at a red-framed photograph of a small boy and a man with mucky blond hair. Blond hair just like Ethan's.

I shuffled the remaining steps to the window. Galloping unicorns, we were up high. Everything looked tiny, like the miniature village at Candy Kingdom.

'Cool, isn't it?' Ethan said, joining me.

'Yes, really cool.'

'That's the River Thames in the distance. We should go to the skatepark on the South Bank sometime.'

I nodded, my eyes still fixed on the glimmering river. 'Have you always lived here, Ethan?'

'Yes,' he said apologetically. 'Dad said Mum deserved better.' He looked out wistfully across London. 'One day I'm going to give it to her.'

The sun shone warm through the glass. I waited for Ethan to continue but he just kept staring out of the window.

'Tell me more about your dad.'

Ethan sat down on the sofa. 'You'd have liked him, Ava. He had a different way of looking at things – like you.' He fiddled in the drawer in the coffee table and took out a flat black object. 'Want to see some photos?'

'Yes, please.' I sat down beside Ethan.

'OK, I'll just order the pizza first.'

Ethan ran his fingers over the black object. It had a screen on it like his phone. He ordered dinner by pressing the images of food. *Oh my curly candy*, I so needed one of those in Biscotti. Just imagine how cool it would be, never having to speak to Cook again.

'Ha, look at this.' Ethan brought up a video

clip of him and his dad. They were on holiday playing this weird game called whack-a-mole. It seemed a bit mean to me, hitting those cute little creatures on the head, but Ethan was happy and I loved hearing his stories about his dad. He had tons of them.

When the pizza finally arrived, we both legged it down the hallway. I got to the door first. I was so excited about paying for the pizza with one of the twenty-pound notes that came with my wallet. I took off the chain and opened the door.

I really wished I'd looked through the spyhole first.

# CHAPTER 20

The Godfather.

I tried to slam the door shut, but it was too late – he'd already jammed his army boot against the frame. He let out a bored sigh like he was being forced to watch opera or something, and pushed the door back. Even with Ethan helping, there was no way we could compete with the bulk of the Godfather. We toppled back into the hallway.

'Right, Maggot, game's up.' The Godfather rested his shoulder against the door frame.

'Queenie wants you 'ome immediately.'

*Uh-oh, this wasn't good.*

'Come on, sooner we're out of here the better. I 'ate coming to this place but I couldn't exactly refuse now, could I? What with being wrong about the unicorns as well.'

'Ava?' Ethan raised his eyebrows. He leant into my ear. 'No wonder you don't like talking about your parents.'

'He's not my dad. He's—'

'Nigel, but you can call me the Godfather.' Nigel stuck his hand out for Ethan to shake. 'Pleased to make your acquaintance. Now come on, Maggot. Before your mother comes and drags you 'ome herself.'

'But—'

'No buts.' The Godfather put his hands on his hips. 'You don't want her going off on one in front of yer little boyfriend 'ere, now do yer?'

*My boyfriend, like ew.*

'Bye then,' Ethan said, his face bright red. 'I'll see you tomorrow.'

The Godfather did a strange wiggle and

pulled his jumpsuit out of his bum. 'Oh, Maggot won't be coming back,' he said.

'But I promised Ethan I'd help him practise his start.'

'Tell that to your mother, Avariella Petulia Winifred Pandoro D'Allessandro of Biscotti. I'm sure she'll be all ears, right after she's chucked you in the dungeon.'

Ethan's eyes widened.

'It's fine,' I said. 'I'd better go.'

Ethan's face was full of questions. Questions I wanted to answer but couldn't. 'It's OK if you can't come tomorrow,' he said. 'I'll understand.'

I nodded. I mean, I knew Ethan would understand before he said it. He was that kind of friend. But that just made the thought of letting him down even harder.

The car park outside the flats was deserted. I kicked a discarded Coke can towards the bin and folded my arms.

'Cheer up, Maggot,' the Godfather said. 'Could have been worse. Could 'ave been your dad who'd found out about yer little rendezvous.'

True, but I was pretty sure Mum was going to have something to say about it too. I was *so* in for it.

The Godfather opened the door to a glittery lime-green car – 'Fiat Panda' said the badge on the back.

'You have a car?'

'Shush,' he said, strapping my BMX to the tartan bike rack. 'You need to be more discreet.'

*Yeah, right.* I climbed into the car, trying to avoid the pink fluffy dice hanging from the mirror. The car wobbled as the Godfather squeezed into the driver's seat.

He looked at his wishometer-watch. 'Going to miss me tea again cause of you. Missus won't be 'appy, I tell yer.'

I wondered if the Godfather's 'missus' was ever happy married to him. He huffed again and started the car with a special key. It spluttered like a dragon with a cold. 'Come on,' he said, patting the control panel. 'That's my girl.'

'Wait,' I said, 'wait!'

Ethan was racing down the steps on his bike. He looked really serious.

'There's something wrong with Ethan.'

The Godfather shook his head and released the brake. 'Godfather waits for no man. And he certainly don't wait for no maggot.'

He pulled out on to the main road where the traffic was doing its usual slow crawl. The man in the car behind us beeped and did a funny wave. He seemed angry for someone who was waving, but the Godfather didn't seem to notice.

'Leave it, Maggot,' he said. 'I told yer, I'm not going back so you can say goodbye to yer boyfriend.'

'How many times do I have to tell you, he is not my boyfriend.'

'Whatever.' The Godfather took his hands off the wheel and raised his palms.

'But I just want to—'

'Stop it. Yer like an ogre with a bone.' The Godfather rummaged in the tray in the car door, muttering as he flung a pair of hiking socks, a mousetrap and a fluorescent pink sweatband on to the back seat. 'I'd be more worried about the mess you've made back 'ome, if I was you. Yer mother is not happy.'

'What mess?'

'You'll find out soon enough. Now shut it and let me concentrate.'

He opened a thin plastic case which had a picture of sweaty people dancing on it. 'That's what I was looking for,' he said, taking out the metal disc and slotting it into the car control

panel. 'I've missed me German techno.'

Oh my giddy goblin, what was this racket? The Godfather held his finger on the volume button and the tiny car began to shake, the drumbeat pulsing through my body and making my teeth chatter. Zingy electronic notes pinged around the car like gunfire. I stuck my fingers in my ears, willing the torture to stop.

Just as I was losing the will to live completely, the car screeched to a stop and I lurched forward. I pulled my fingers out of my ears and peeled open an eye.

'Out yer get,' said the Godfather, switching off the music. 'Go on, yer mother's waiting for yer on the other side.'

I stepped out on to the pavement. 'But where am I?'

The Godfather rolled his eyes. 'Down the stairs,' he said, pointing to a gap in the wall. 'Turn left when you get to the bottom and ride as fast as you can with no stopping. You'll know the portal when you see it.'

He took his wand out and pointed it towards

the back of the car. My BMX clanged to the floor.

'But aren't you coming?'

''Course not,' the Godfather said. 'It's teatime, and I've got a date with a metre-long hotdog at Camden Market. Then I'm off to see Kev about this stirring in his chakra crystals.'

'Pardon?' *The Godfather was talking in riddles again.*

'Never you mind,' he said, tapping his nose. 'Ask your mother about Kevin. Or on second thoughts, maybe not.'

*Whatever!* He was so annoying. Next he'd be spouting the stupid nursery rhyme again.

He turned on the engine. 'See you around, Maggot. And don't forget to secure the portal. We don't want anyone else following you through.'

# CHAPTER 21

Jumping jelly beans, I don't think I'll ever get used to portal travel. I'd mastered the landing – I hardly ever hurt my bum now – but I still felt like I'd been inside a candyfloss machine every time I went through the gateway. I leant back against the giant stone fireplace in the banqueting room, willing the swaying to stop.

Through the fingers of violet mist, I saw a figure. A figure with bizarrely big hair. Troll poop! It was Mum.

'Avariella,' she said. 'You've been a very

naughty girl.'

'I'm sorry, I didn't know—'

The giant gong in the Grand Hall boinged, its vibrations echoing through the floor. Rapid footsteps joined the echoes.

'Save it, sweetie.' Mum wheeled my BMX behind the pile of stacked banqueting chairs and pulled me towards the spiral staircase. 'We've got a meeting to spy on.'

From the balcony above the Council Chambers we had a perfect view of the platform where Dad and the ten knights of the Tavolo Rettangolare were holding their meeting.

'What's Tufty Troutbottom doing here?' Mum said, widening the gap in the plush velvet curtains.

Good question. Tufty is famous throughout the kingdom for being the seventh descendent of the Seventh Dwarf. Dad says he makes far too big a deal about this. Personally, I don't like to judge but, put it this way, all of Tufty's seven children are called Snow White. The dwarf was perched on an umpire stool at the far end of the table, his legs dangling uncomfortably above the foot bar. He crossed his arms over his pudding-shaped belly and bowed his head at Dad.

'Welcome, Tufty.' Dad pointed his quill at his chief knight. 'Louseylot, please commence.'

'Yes, sire.' Sir Louseylot had obviously had his hair done again. It was all glossy and bouncy. He held up a gold-framed painting. 'Is this the woman you saw, Tufty?'

'Yes, sire.'

'Speak up, man.' Dad rested his elbows on the mahoosive polished wood table and leant forward.

Tufty stroked his long white beard 'Yes, sire. I swear on Eric here's life, it was her.' He fumbled in his pocket and took out a long mouse-like animal which he held up in the air.

'Put the weasel away, Tufty!' Dad looked out at the rows of empty pews below the platform. 'Now tell me again what occurred.'

'Well, I was out at the cornfields beyond the Black Forest. My old hip was playing up. I'm two hundred and two, you know.'

'Yes. And what happened at the cornfields?'

'It was breakfast time. I knows it because my stomach was rumbling. I have to eat regular because of my ulcer—'

'Tufty.'

Tufty leant forward. He scratched his ankle and Eric the weasel popped out of his trouser leg. He caught him by the tail and put him back in his pocket.

'I smelt somethin', I did,' he continued. 'Something sweet. I thoughts my old mind was playing tricks on me. But then I saw 'im, Alun, the sherbet dragon. I waved—'

'Time is precious, Tufty, please.'

'Sorry, sire. The dragon was with the Black Sorceress.'

All of the knights started to talk at once.

'Order, gentlemen!' Dad banged his fist on the table and the knights were silent again. 'Are you sure, Tufty?' he continued.

'Oh, yes, sire. Absolutely. She was wearing funny clothes, but I'd recognize the Lady Odette anywheres.'

*Odette.* I grabbed Mum's arm. That was the name of the creepy woman from the Other World.

Dad broke the silence by shuffling his papers. 'Thank you, Tufty,' he said. 'That will be all. Please remember that your discretion in this matter is much appreciated. It is essential that we do not cause unnecessary alarm.'

'Oh, don't worry 'bout that,' Tufty said, looking at his feet. 'Don't see a soul for days sometimes. Nobody bothers to visit old Tufty.'

Dad glared at Periwinkle, who rushed over to escort Tufty from the chambers. Their footsteps echoing in the rafters, they made their way between the carved stone columns and out of the door.

'That's the second reported sighting, sire,' said Sir Louseylot. 'Both completely independent of each other. I'll alert the Fairy Council.'

'No.' Dad pressed the tips of his fingers together. 'The sighting has not yet been confirmed.'

'But sire, what with the bluestone awakening—'

*Bluestone? Wasn't that what Mum and Dad were arguing about in the carriage?* Mum's eyes gave nothing away.

'These things happen in cycles.' Dad pushed away his papers. 'The increased activity could just be the stone regulating itself.'

'Yes, sire.' Sir Louseylot glanced around the table. 'But with your permission perhaps it wouldn't hurt to have their people on the look-out for your sister.'

*Like, what! My ears must be broken.* I turned to Mum, but she shook her head and pushed me into the shadow of the wall.

'Not now,' she said.

I wasn't going to argue. She looked about as happy as a teenage ogre who'd been forced to take a shower.

'Oh, Bertrand,' she called, pulling the curtain back dramatically. 'It's time to wake up and smell the wart blossom.'

Dad's throne scraped against the wooden floor. His troll-poop face was a classic.

'You know Odette has always had a fascination with that dragon,' Mum continued. 'Every-one knows it was her silly games that messed up his sherbet valve.'

'Really, Sophia. How many times must I say it? The portals were sealed. There is no way my sister could have returned.'

I stared at Mum, suddenly cold. So, it was true. The creepy woman really was my auntie! How could they keep something like this from me?

'Oh, there's always a way,' she continued. 'Believe me.'

'Balderdash! Your words have no substance.'

'You're a fool, Bertrand.'

'Sophia! I will hear no more of this matter.'

'A fool. And a fool and his kingdom are soon parted.'

The knights suddenly seemed very interested in the tabletop. Some of them were holding in sniggers.

Mum chopped the air with her hand. 'So, when you're ready, sweetcheeks, I could do with a word. In private!'

# CHAPTER 22

I found Mum eventually in the far corner of the library, the rolling ladder used to reach the highest bookshelves just behind her. She looked up from the leather-bound logbook she was reading and slammed it shut.

'I hope you're happy, young lady. Because your father's most certainly not.'

Here we go. I knew I should have just put my BMX away in my closet and gone to bed. I crossed my arms and prepared myself for the earbashing. But Mum just did her disappointed stare. It's the same disappointed stare all grown-ups do when they want to make you feel guilty.

'We have to tell him,' I said pulling a chair out and sitting down opposite Mum.

'Tell him what.'

'Odette, she's been following me.'

'You'll say nothing, young lady. Your father is furious enough as it is. If he finds out I've been allowing you to use the portal too, I'll never hear the last of it.'

I touched my throat. 'You knew?'

'Of course I knew. Who do you think told Nigel to give you your bicycle? Nothing gets past my Other World surveillance.'

I coughed. I mean, what about Odette for a start?

'I didn't have the heart to stop you,' she continued. 'What with that terrible Hornet-Boules and your dad breathing down your neck every five minutes.' She leant across the desk and took my hand. 'I know what it feels like to need that escape. Your father is not an easy man.'

*Like, hello. Ten out of ten for observation, Mother.*

'That's why I asked Nigel to open the portal in the first place. Still amazes me he managed to break the charm. Just shows what a man can achieve when driven by the offer of a royal appointment and an unlimited supply of squirrel.'

Mum turned back to her logbook. She ran her index finger over the gold letters that spelt out the title: *The Protectors*. The book shrank to the size of a matchbox. She put it in her pocket.

'But you were supposed to follow the rules. The Godfather assures me, he spelt them out clearly.'

Mum pointed her finger at me and started to spout the same daft nursery rhyme the God-father had spouted when he gave me my bike:

*It starts with a kick,*
*A kick of the heel,*
*With a bit of spit, it opens no big deal,*
*But do make sure to secure it again,*
*By tapping twice and counting to ten.*

I felt a funny feeling in my tummy.

'Honestly,' Mum continued, 'if there's one thing you should be used to it's following rules.'

The funny feeling grew worse. I'd thought it was just a silly Godfather thing – the magic love their daft rhymes and traditions. 'But Mum, I didn't realize...'

'You never do, Avariella. But realize this. I don't want you going anywhere near that portal again.'

'But what about Ethan?'

'No buts. Odette is dangerous. We have reason to believe this is not her first trip through the portal. I want you here where I can keep an eye on you.'

I shook my head and huffed.

'And don't look at me that way, missy. You brought this on yourself with your carelessness.'

'Well, maybe if someone had told me I had an EVIL auntie running around in the Other World, I'd have been more careful.'

'I seriously doubt it, Avariella. Your listening skills have never been your strong point. You have to learn to take responsibility for your actions.'

*Ouch!* Like, say it how it is, Mum. Next she'd be throwing the expectations at me like Dad and Hornet-Boules. Well, there were things I expected too – the truth, for a start. I mean, Odette, the Other World and now all this talk of some weird bluestone, what else had they been keeping from me?

'Oh, don't get upset, sweetie.' Mum's voice was softer now. 'I suppose you've just sped up the inevitable, really. Odette was always going to come back and take her revenge on your father for banishing her.'

What was the point? As usual Mum just didn't get it.

'Don't worry, your dad might be trying to keep it all low-key, but Nigel and Kevin are on the case. They'll have Odette rounded up and packed off again before you know it. Kevin can do marvellous things with those chakra crystals of his. He once tracked a stray ogre right across the Sahara Desert without anyone in the Other World raising an eyelid. Herbert, his name was. Herbert the Hungry.'

*Yeah, right.* If this Kevin was half as dim as the Godfather, we were seriously doomed.

'Now off you go.' Mum made a sweeping motion with her hand. 'You just stay out of trouble and leave things to my boys. And I mean it, Avariella. Stay away from the portal or I'll feed you to Herbert the Hungry myself.'

# CHAPTER 23

I wrapped the blanket around my legs, the flickering oil lamp casting long shadows around my chambers. I stared down at the BMX book I'd borrowed from Ethan. I must have read the same line about ten times now. It just wasn't going in. I thought about getting back in bed, but there was like zero point. No way was I going back to sleep with everything that was whirling around in my head. And now on top of Mum and Dad's skeletons, I was banned from going to the Kingdom of Camden. No matter how much

I tried, I couldn't get Mum to change her mind.

I sighed and pulled back the velvet drape. The first sun was beginning to rise and the sky was the colour of blueberries. I looked out across the shadowy kingdom – the kingdom that would one day be mine. I'd never felt so lonely in my life. I really needed a cuddle from Jeb, but Mum said he wasn't allowed to sleep in my room for a month as part of my punishment for not sealing the portal. How could she do that to us? Poor Jeb. He looked so sad going to bed with grumpy Bertie. He just didn't understand.

Ethan wouldn't understand either. I couldn't bear the thought of him thinking I'd just given up on our friendship. Or what if he thought something bad had happened to me? He'd be so worried. I had to go and see him one more time, tell him the truth, even if he didn't believe me—

Footsteps thundered along the corridor outside my chambers. A fist thumped against my bedroom door.

'Yes?'

'Lady Jemima Jeopardy here, Your Highness.

The King asked me to check on you.'

'I'm fine.' *I like so didn't need a knight in my room right now.*

'I'm to take you downstairs immediately,' she said.

I climbed down from the window seat and fastened my dressing gown.

'Immediately,' she repeated.

More footsteps, this time they were accompanied by urgent voices.

'Ma'am, I'm coming in.'

Sword in one hand, her unicorn-embossed shield in the other, Lady Jemima Jeopardy kicked the door open and stormed into the room her thick, waist-length plaits swinging from side to side. She touched my arm like she was making sure I was real, then searched under the bed and in the closet. Scanning the room, she ran over to the window and poked the curtains with her sword.

'Sorry to alarm you, Your Highness,' she said, straightening her silver helmet. 'Only there's been a security breach.'

'In the castle?' *How was that even possible? Nothing could get past the security charm – family and invited guests only.*

'Yes, Your Highness, in the castle. Your parents are waiting in the study. Hurry, please.'

And then it hit me like the stench of Swamp Diavolo – thanks to me there was a *new* family member in town. Odette.

'Bertie and Jeb,' I said, the words catching in my throat. 'We need to check on them.'

Lady Jemima Jeopardy blew her blonde fringe out of her eyes. 'My instructions are to take you straight downstairs.'

This didn't look good. There were guards all along the corridor. None of them would look at me. I glanced past them, towards Bertie's chambers, where there were fairies in white coats dusting down the door frame with a violet powder. Through the gap in the door, I caught a glimpse of the Godfather's silver jumpsuit. I put my head down and sped along the corridor to the study.

In the dim light of the French windows, Mum and Dad looked almost ghostly. Mum was wearing her long green dressing gown, Doreen curled up in her teddy-bear pyjamas at her feet. My tummy churned like the buttermaid's barrel – Mum never came downstairs in her nightclothes. Louseylot was in the study too. They were bending over the table looking at a map, Dad barking out orders.

'Make haste,' he said. 'Raise the alarm across the kingdom.'

'Your Highness.' Sir Louseylot bowed his head at me. His armour clanking, he opened the French windows and made his way towards the stables.

'Oh Ava, thank goodness.'

I pulled away from Mum's bear hug. 'Please, Mum. Where are Bertie and Jeb—'

*Thwack!* The heavy wooden door slammed against the wall, and Great-aunt Maude forced her walking frame into the room.

'She's taken them,' she yelled. 'Little Bertie and the curly dog.' Maude, who to Dad's obvious horror was wearing just her long lacy knicker-bockers and a corset, rummaged around in the pillowcase hanging from her wooden walking frame and pulled out her jam jar.

'See? The eye, it's weeping.'

'Mum?' But already I knew it was true.

Mum nodded. 'I'm sorry, Avariella.'

*What had I done?*

Maude gave me a sad, gummy smile. 'They're OK,' she said. 'Now, help me, Umbrella.'

I scurried over to Maude. She handed me the bright-pink pet-carry bag that was over her shoulder. It looked very *Other World*.

'Wait, and this.'

Screwing up my nose, I took the jam jar. *Like, eugh!* The eye was swollen to twice its normal size, and angry red veins laced the white fleshy bit. The fluid that surrounded the eyeball was tinged pink.

'Put it on the table,' Maude said, pushing her walking frame across the room towards Dad. With her beige hairnet and no teeth in, she looked disturbingly like Bertie's tortoise-seat.

The warning bell in the North Tower rang out, triggering the sounding of bells across the kingdom. Dad pushed the jam jar away and shook his head. 'Sharp as ever, Aunt Maude, I see.'

'Oh, shut yer cakehole and listen to your old auntie for once.' Maude dug around in her pillowcase and pulled out a flowery china teacup and some tiny ear defenders. 'Because you might think you know it all, but I know where you'll find them.' She handed me the ear defenders. 'Now, child, cover Tyson's ears, and whatever you do don't let him see the cup.'

I rooted around in the pet carrier and pulled out Tyson. The ear defenders fell straight off. Which was hardly surprising given he was a teabag with a distinct lack of body parts. *Ears, my bubblegum!* I shoved the defenders and Tyson back into the bag and zipped it up. Maude wasn't looking anyway. She was staring into the teacup.

'Breaks my heart to do this in front of Tyson, but what he doesn't know won't hurt him. I should give tea up really, but I keep forgetting.'

'Really, Maude, we don't have time for this tomfoolery.'

'Do as your aunt says and shut it.' Mum threw Dad the evils big-style. 'Are you forgetting why she carries the charmed eyeball in the first place?'

Maude thrust the cup towards Dad. 'Look.'

'Tea leaves.' Dad folded his arms. 'How extraordinary, given it's a teacup.'

'Shush.' said Mum. 'Have some respect for the old magic.'

'Oh, don't mind him,' Maude said. 'He's never been able to see what's staring him in the face, let alone the future.' She shifted the cup towards Mum. 'See the line?'

'Yes,' Mum said.

'Well, that line's a river. It's bubbly, so that means it's the Limonadi River.'

Dad tutted. He looked out of the window towards the stables and tutted again.

Mum's forehead crinkled – she didn't look convinced either – but she continued to listen to Maude.

'And those two tea leaves there. See them –

smaller than all the others? Well, they're Bertie and the curly dog.'

'Poppycock,' Dad said. 'I'm going to check on the knights. They should have left by now.'

'Poppycock, yerself!' Maude put her cup away and picked up the jam jar. She stared at the pulsating eyeball. 'I'm telling you that boy is on his way to the Limonadi River. The tea leaves never lie!'

# CHAPTER 24

**M**um waited while Great-aunt Maude made her way out of the study. I'd offered to carry Tyson back to the caravan for her, but Maude said she could manage just fine by herself, thank you very much.

'She's as stubborn as a minotaur,' Mum said. 'Come on, let's go and find out what's going on with the knights.'

She wrapped her dressing gown tight around her and, Doreen running along in front, head-butting the startled chickens, we made our way to the stables.

Dad was standing in the doorway with Sir Louseylot.

'Sophia,' he said. 'A new peril strikes!' He pointed at his black stallion, Calvin. The horse was standing as still a gargoyle, his huge tongue hanging limply from his mouth, black foam frothing from his nostrils.

Mum ran her hand down Calvin's neck. 'Have you sent for the Godfather?'

'Someone mention me name?' The Godfather waved at us from the rafters where he was hanging by his feet like a vampire. He swung forwards, spinning around in an elaborate somersault before landing next to Mum.

'They've been charmed, they 'ave.' He poked a grey mare called Ethel in the eye. She didn't even blink. 'Used the wart blossom, I reckon. Every 'orse in Bicotti's down, according to Bob.'

'Any fool can see it's a charm,' said Dad. 'The question is, what are you going to do about it?'

The Godfather crossed his arms. 'Nowt.'

'What?'

'I need violas and they're outta season.'

'Out of season!'

''Course, I could get some dried ones, but there's no point—'

'Now listen here,' Dad said, curling his fists into tight balls. His face was so red I was worried his head might explode. Which would have been kind of cool but it wasn't going to help the situation.

And for once I couldn't blame Dad for being angry. Bertie and Jeb were in great danger and the Godfather was being super-awkward. Thankfully Mum knew how to work him.

'Bertrand, dear,' she said. 'Let Nigel finish. After all, he's the expert in these matters.'

The Godfather's smile stretched from one gigantic ear to the other. He pulled down the zip on his jumpsuit just in case we'd missed the gold medallion.

'As I was sayin'. There's no point cause it's a time-limited spell. By the time I get hold of the violas and soak them in newts' wee, it'll 'ave worn off. The knights could 'ave walked to the

159

cornfields by then.'

'Louseylot!' Mum clicked her fingers. 'You heard what Nigel said. Summon your knights and commence the search on foot. Odette is playing games with us and we have no option but to play along.'

Louseylot looked at Dad.

'Keep to the plan,' he said. 'I'll send the horses when they're recovered.'

'But – Aunt Maude.' I tugged Mum's sleeve.

'I'm afraid your dad's right, love. We can't put all our faith in the hands of a split teabag.' Mum glared at Sir Louseylot. 'I said, *go*!' She clutched her hand to her chest. 'And be sure to spread word across the kingdom – the Black Sorceress has returned and she wants revenge.'

# CHAPTER 25

Like, no way, I'd been sent to my room again. Honestly, Rapunzel got out more than I did lately. She'd been lied to all her life too. I peeled off the tissue paper and put another chocolate lime in my mouth, but even my favourite sweets were not going to fix this. Bertie and Jeb were missing and it was all my fault . . .

Well, maybe not quite *all* my fault. I just didn't understand why nobody had told me about Odette. Mum said Dad was embarrassed – she'd brought great shame on the family with her

EVIL plans for multi-world domination – but what kind of an excuse was that? Sure, it was pretty cringetastic, but Bertie reads encyclopedias for pleasure and thinks homework's the best thing since marshmallows. Like, deal with it, Dad.

There was a gust of wind and my window banged shut. I climbed up on the window seat to open it again, catching sight of Sir Louseylot and his knights clanking along in their heavy armour. *Like, how slow.* They hadn't even reached the Black Forest yet. Without their horses, it was going to take them for ever to find Bertie and Jeb.

I chewed my thumb and looked out beyond the knights to the cornfields. Bertie would be OK. He was like Mr Sensible after all – which was extremely annoying when you wanted him to play catch-the-grumpy-fairy or climb trees with you – but was no doubt useful in a kidnap situation. He'd know to stay calm and not upset Odette. The knights would come to him . . . eventually.

Growling griffins, they were so slow. Every

now and again they'd break into a clumsy trot, but then they'd have to stop and walk again because of their heavy armour. I could be so much quicker on my bike. And there was far less chance of Odette seeing me coming. I mean, you could probably hear that lot clunking in Camden. Odette was EVIL but she wasn't stupid. What was needed was an element of surprise. Something unexpected. And no one expects a princess to be a knight in shining BMX gear and go kick her EVIL auntie's butt! *It was perfect!*

I ran over to my closet. Battling lace and silk and taffeta, I fought my way through the wall of pink dresses to my BMX. I'd been worried the Godfather would confiscate it, but thankfully he'd been too busy trying to hunt Odette down. And with Mum having sent him to Camden, to make sure my EVIL auntie hadn't taken Bertie and Jeb there, this was my chance to sneak my bike out and go and put things right.

Except it wasn't.

Not with Lady Jemima Jeopardy standing

outside my chambers. Good job I'd checked the corridor before I got changed into my BMX gear. In the name of the good goblin, how was I supposed to sneak my bike out now! Unless . . .

I ran back over to the window. Doreen was on her back legs, chewing the blackened bark on the tree-trunk bridge the servants used as a shortcut across the moat. *Brilliant, Do-Do.* That was my way out of here. That, and the window.

I unhooked my rucksack from my bike and pulled out my jeans and T-shirt. Eyes fixed on the heavy gold cord used to tie back the curtains, I got changed. Pausing to put the chocolate limes in my pocket, I ripped the cord down from the iron hooks, knotted the pieces together and tied it to my BMX. *Easy does it.* I lifted my bike on to the stone sill where it wobbled half in and half out of the room.

Yikes. It was a long way down. The cord was nowhere near long enough to reach the ground. But if I could somehow swing my BMX to the side of the window, I could drop it into the bushes. Slowly I began to release the cord, biting my lip as the weight of the frame dragged it through my fingers and my bike clanged against the wall, the sound echoing around the gardens. Jumping jelly beans, I hope nobody heard.

Steadying myself against the window frame, I pulled back on the cord and looked around. There was no one there, but my bike was still a long way from the ground. I gulped – the drop seemed bigger every time I looked down. I shook my head. I couldn't think about falling. Bertie and Jeb needed me. I might not be able to change the fact I'd let Odette back in the kingdom, but maybe if I found my brother and dog, I could make everything all right. I *had* to make everything all right.

Arms trembling, I swung my BMX towards the shrubs and let go of the cord. It landed on top of a large holly bush, wobbling there for a second before hitting the ground with a thud. *You can do this, Ava*, I told myself. I persuaded my leg out of the window. The other leg followed. Gripping the top of the window frame, I shuffled along the sill until I reached the thick ivy that grew up the castle wall. The vines were rough on my rope-burnt hands, but they made an awesome ladder. So long as I didn't look down, I'd be fine.

And I was.

My bike was fine too. Dropping it in the bushes was a good move. There was a dent in the frame but nothing major. I untied the cord and gave my BMX a final check. Climbing on, I noticed something silver on the ground: my bike pump. I picked it up, and ran my finger over the P emblem, remembering how the Godfather had made such a fuss about keeping it with me all the time. I put it in my rucksack and climbed on to my bike. It was time to get my dog and brother back.

# CHAPTER 26

*ikes.* I pulled back hard on the brakes and skidded to a stop. The tree-trunk bridge across the moat was much higher than I remembered and it was covered in patches of furry green mould which looked mega-slippy. I rested my chin on the handlebars and studied the giant log, wishing I'd gone dirt biking with Ant and Cleo. Maybe I should just forget it altogether...

*Galloping unicorns, Ava.* I kicked the ground in frustration. *Stop being such a wimpy knickers.*

The log was no big deal. I just had to get enough lift and hold my bike steady. Glancing back over my shoulder, I edged backwards, catching sight of Doreen running around in the flower beds. She was still wearing her teddy-bear pyjama top. She bleated and raced across the grass towards me. So much for slipping away quietly. I needed to get a shift on. I sped towards the tree.

Holding the pedals flat, I pulled back hard on my handlebars and lifted my front wheel on to the smooth bark. Eyes fixed in front of me, I shifted my weight to the front of the bike so the back wheel followed. I focused on the bushes straight ahead and stayed steady all the way across the giant log. *Easy!* Sorry, Doreen, but this BMX princess was out of here!

OK, so that made me sound like a show-off, but trust me, by the time I reached the centre of Amaretti, I didn't feel so sure of things. It was totally freaky: no shoppers carrying baskets overloaded with griffin eggs and dragon cabbage, no red-faced mums and dads calling the kids in for cake-o'clock; and not a single crazy honey-fox barking at the wooden carts. Even the cloud aardvarks were hiding from Odette.

So why did it feel like I was being followed? My shoulders tense, I checked behind me again, scanning the empty doorways, but there was definitely nobody there. Above me, the wooden sign outside the tavern swung back and forth on its rusty hinges. Why was it moving when there was no wind? I wasn't hanging around to find out. I pegged it down the cobbled street towards the edge of town.

Galloping unicorns, I had to pull myself together. I couldn't allow myself to get spooked by every little thing. *Don't get distracted* is what Ethan would say. Concentrate on the trick. But no matter how much I tried to keep my mind on the overgrown path, it kept wandering back to the scary stories about the Black Forest. Stories that would make you wet the bed. Sure, you haven't wet the bed for like ever, but trust me, you would if you heard what happened to Billy Bumble.

And then there it was in front of me, a wall of

trees so high it hurt my neck to look up at the canopy. Chewing my thumbnail, I peered through the ancient tree trunks at the cart track. Would my bike be OK on this sort of uneven trail? And what about all the terrible stories? Billy Bumble wasn't the only child the Black Forest had stolen. But I couldn't just leave Bertie to Odette. Especially when this was all my fault. It was me she'd followed back through the portal; it was me she should have taken. Ignoring the weird feeling in my tummy, I took a deep breath and pedalled forward. It would be fine, just fine, so long as I stuck to the cart tracks. I mean, a few months ago I couldn't even ride a bike and now I was learning air tricks.

The forest lived up to its name. Shivering in the grey mist that wrapped itself around my ankles, I paused and let my eyes adjust to the darkness. The trees were packed so closely together their giant roots grew above the ground. In the dim misty light, they looked like giant woody fingers trying to block my way. I wouldn't let them.

I rode on, flinching at the touch of the dragon's-beard growing above my head. It was everywhere, hanging from the branches like a cotton-wool veil. *Think of nice things*, I told myself, picking it out of my hair. *Nice things like Jeb and profiteroles. It will be OK.*

Maybe. But the forest wasn't going to make this easy for me. The roots were slipperier than a sugar eel and the brambles that grew in between the trees pulled at my T-shirt and scratched my arms. How could this be the main route into the forest? There was no way a cart would make it through here. I must have taken a wrong turn.

I retraced my route along the path. But there was no other way to go. My cheeks burning with frustration, I turned round again, attacking the tree roots with everything I had. Tree roots, brambles, dragon's-beard – by the good goblin, none of it was going to stop me.

I had to find Bertie and Jeb.

# CHAPTER 27

I was deep in the forest now. The trees were packed less tightly together and I was able to pick up speed. My mind wandered to Ethan. I couldn't stand never seeing him again. Maybe, if I put things right, I'd be allowed one more trip to Camden ... But for now, I had to concentrate on finding Bertie. Shredding like an Olympic multi-gold medallist, I put my head down and tuned in to the forest.

For the first time, I noticed birdsong. Beams of light broke through the canopy, warming my skin. They made the dewdrops sparkle like diamonds. They were pretty. So pretty. I followed the dancing lights further into the forest, a warm feeling in my tummy like I'd just drunk a hot chocolate. I was smiling so much my mouth hurt. There was music too. I hummed along. Lifting the front wheel of my bike, I did a wheelie. And a bunny hop. I was so happy I was practically glowing – I wanted to laugh and dance and hug someone.

The music grew louder. Through the trees, I could see a clearing, emerald-green grass dotted with flowers. I had to get to it . . . There was a high-pitched bleat accompanied by a shooting pain in my calf. *Doreen!* Her mane was standing up and her eyes were round and white. She released her pincer-like grip on my leg and bleated at the sky.

*What was she doing here?*

She bleated again – an ear-piercing cry some-where between a goat and a strangled piglet. *Really, Do-Do, what's with the squealing . . . ?*

And then it hit me, hard in the face, like a

bewitched kipper: forest sprites. How could I have been so stupid?

'How dare you,' I said, wagging my finger at the dancing lights. 'I am Princess Avariella Petulia Winifred Pandoro D'Allessandro of Biscotti, and by order of the Fairy Council, all fairy folk must obey my father's command—'

'Sweetheart.' A sprite with bright blue eyes, who looked like a mini-version of the chiselled-featured movie stars in Kaye's gossip magazines, burst from one of the lights. 'Now don't be like that, we're just having a little fun.'

'Do not call me sweetheart.'

'*Babe*, then.' The sprite flew closer. He smelt of chocolate blossom. 'Look, how were we supposed to know you're a princess when you're dressed like a chimney sweep? A pretty girl like you deserves silk and velvet. Have you seen Cinderella's new look? I could put you in touch with her stylist.'

'Oh, please!' I batted the sprite away with my hand. 'Come on, Do-Do.'

Doreen bared her teeth at the sprite. She trotted to the overgrown path that led away from the hollow.

'Your loss, sweetheart. We're done with you anyway.'

'What do you mean, done with me.'

'Just a little distraction, darling, nothing too scary,' said the sprite in a voice that now sounded just like Odette. 'Leave the petrifying for the knights.'

'What?'

'Oh, nothing.' He nodded behind me. 'Think you'd better go check on your microcorn.'

'Doreen!' I kicked my pedal into position. 'Here, now.'

But Doreen kept on running. She disappeared under the canopy of a giant sugar-star bush.

Leaves crunched underfoot and the bush rustled.

A high-pitched bleat echoed through the forest.

'Doreen!'

But it wasn't Doreen who came fighting her way out of the bushes.

Oh my curly candy, Mum was going to kill me. Herbert the Hungry may as well sharpen his knives right now because the ogre's stewpot was definitely the way I was heading once she found out Ethan was here!

Yes, Ethan. Tall skinny dude with mad sticky-up hair. Tall skinny dude from the Other World! Here in Biscotti. I was *so* in for it.

I put my hands on his shoulders and pushed

him back into the bushes. 'You have to go back. Now!'

'Nice to see you too,' Ethan said, edging his bike forward. He pulled a twig covered in silver-star blossom from the spokes.

'I'm sorry, Ethan. But if my mum catches you here, we've both had it.'

'What's going on, Ava? What is this place?'

'No time to explain. You just have to trust me. It's too dangerous for you here.'

Ethan scratched the back of his neck. 'Is this one of your weird role-playing things, because if it is, I'm not happy.'

'Just go home, Ethan.'

Ethan caught hold of my T-shirt. 'And how exactly am I supposed to do that?'

I pulled free from his grip but I stayed put. I mean, he kind of had a point. I wasn't sure I could find my way out of the forest either.

'How did you get here, Ethan?'

'I followed that Godfather bloke. I was worried, the way he dragged you away like that, so I went to tell the others. See if they'd help me look for you. I saw him near Camden Lock and followed him along the canal. That's when it got really weird. Like, what's going on, Ava?'

I sighed. 'Do you really want to know? Because you won't believe me.'

Ethan nodded.

'OK. You've travelled through a portal to a different world where my brother's been captured by a dark sorceress who also happens to be my EVIL auntie. She like totally hates my dad and is seeking revenge because he banished her. It's the biggest thing that's happened in Biscotti since my grandad destroyed the purple yeti.'

'*What?* Have you lost it altogether!'

'Told you you wouldn't believe me.' I took the chocolate limes out of my pocket. 'Sweet? I should probably save them for my unicorn really, but we need to keep our energy up.'

# CHAPTER 28

F riends, Biscottians, countrymen lend me your ear plugs *please*! Ethan was totally doing my head in. He just couldn't get his head around the whole magic thing and was spewing out questions like a bewitched porridge pot. All that time lost chasing those stupid lights and now I was wasting more time trying to convince Ethan we weren't playing some sort of virtual reality game. I had to get to my brother. And fast.

Like things weren't hard enough with the mud, the monster tree roots and Ethan's constant assault on my ears, I now had Doreen in my ruck-sack. She'd been slowing me down too much, stopping every two minutes to eat the wild garlic that grew in the gaps between the trees. The stuff was everywhere. Its pungent scent tickled my nose and made my eyes water.

'Are you OK?' Ethan said, pulling his bike up beside me.

'Fine. I've just got sensitive eyes – it's a princess thing.'

Ethan shook his head. He still didn't believe my story – despite the fact he'd arrived here by portal!

'Hey look at this tree.' He slowed and reached up to touch one of the branches trailing above our heads.

With their downy leaves, they reminded me of feather boas. If I wasn't on a mission to save my brother from my EVIL auntie, I'd have broken one off and worn it around my neck.

'Come on, Ethan,' I said. 'I told you. We need to hurry.'

Ethan saluted me. 'Let us make haste, fair maiden.'

*Like, whatever.* I rode on. When I looked back over my shoulder Ethan was lying on the floor.

'Ethan, what are you doing now?'

*Oops*, now I was on the floor too. Doreen bleated and butted my shoulder, trying to get out of the rucksack. I took it off and tipped her out.

'Ava?' Ethan scrambled towards me on his knees, pointing at the tree. 'Tell me that's not really happening.'

# CHAPTER 29

*L*ike, what? My bike was being dragged along
the ground by a tree root. Growling griffins,
it had to be those pesky sprites again. Their
silly games were getting so tiring. I raced over to
the feather-boa tree and stamped down on the
root as hard as I could.

'Ouch, that hurt.'

The voice seemed to come from the tree. I put
my hands on my hips and tutted. Like, really, did
those sprites think I had candyfloss between my
ears? I bent down to untangle my bike – but the

tree lifted it up into its branches

'Just quit with the games, you lot!' I kicked the tree in frustration.

'Why, you ruffian!' The tree shook and a storm of black-and-white plumes tumbled to the ground.

I put my hand over my open mouth. Oh my curly candy, it wasn't the sprites at all. The tree was a magpie tree. Like, *wowzas*. I'd heard of magpie trees, but I'd never seen one. They only grew deep in the Black Forest.

'Scoundrel,' the tree continued, 'terrorizing an innocent tree!' He parted his lower branches and a pair of beady eyes peered out at me. 'And please control that animal. Its nibbling is most discourteous.'

I picked up Doreen. She still had a piece of tree root in her teeth.

'Innocent!' I said. 'You've stolen our bikes.'

'Stolen . . . ?' The tree sighed. 'I prefer to call it collecting.'

I rolled my eyes at Ethan, who was still on his knees making a weird noise somewhere between a choke and a cry.

'Oh dear,' the tree continued. 'I suppose it might seem that way. What to say? It's in the sap, old girl. When I see something shiny, I have to have it.'

I smiled – I couldn't help it. With his beaky nose, he really did look like a magpie.

'By golly.' The tree covered his eyes with a feathery branch. 'I thought I had my obsession under control. Forgive me, child, for it appears I'm beaten.'

'Erg, whatever,' I said, finally able to get a word in. 'We just want our bikes back. Come on, Ethan.'

Ethan didn't move. He just kept staring at the tree.

The tree stared back at him. 'Jeepers, is your friend OK? Have I upset him with my discourtesy?'

The tree made a weird wailing sound and started to cry. Doreen joined in. She was bleating so much she shook.

'And now I've upset your microcorn too. This day grows ever darker.'

I looked at my watch. I didn't want to be rude, but as much as I'd have loved to help the tree with its personal issues, my brother and dog had been captured by an EVIL sorceress and that kind of took priority.

'Well,' I said, 'no big deal. If you could just pass our bikes down, we'll be on our way.'

But the tree was too busy going off on one to hear me. Tears rushed down its trunk, forming puddles on the floor.

'There, there,' I said, patting it. 'It's OK.'

I felt weird patting a tree, but patting stopped Bertie crying when Mum did it, and I didn't know what else to do. Patting didn't work for the tree, though. Maybe I should just change the subject?

'Can you please help me, Mr Tree?' I said, wiping my wet hands on my jeans. 'I'm trying to get to the cornfields—'

'The cornfields?' The tree quivered. It pointed one of its branches at me and waved it from side to side. 'Why, I beseech you, do not venture there.'

'Are they far?' I so didn't have time for the tree's amateur dramatics.

'Far, no. But it is a dangerous journey.' The tree lowered its voice. 'A danger at least trebled by the presence of the Black Sorceress.'

A branch cracked in the distance, the noise sending a flurry of birds into the darkening sky. Ethan looked behind him into the trees. He made a sound like Dad when he's just seen Mum's shopping receipts, and finally he stood up.

'We must be careful,' said the tree. 'She has friends everywhere. The dark force is again stirring.'

I touched the back of my neck where the hairs stood up. *Just a little distraction, darling.* I hadn't given it too much thought at the time – what with Doreen disappearing – but there was definitely something funny going on with those sprites. Mum said Odette was playing with us – were the sprites' tricks part of her game too? And more to the point, right now, was the magpie tree one of her distractions?

'Like, thanks for the warning,' I said. 'But just

give us our bikes back please.'

The tree looked around again, his voice now a whisper. 'Please, take heed. You must return home without delay. For I saw the sorceress with my very own eyes just a few hours ago.'

*A few hours ago.* If the tree was speaking the truth, we were close, so close. 'Come on Ethan.'

The tree sighed, a flurry of black plumes tumbling to the floor along with our bikes. 'As you wish. But I implore you to take care. For fear can turn even the most noble towards the darkness.'

# CHAPTER 30

O K, I like totally got it. A talking tree harping
on about a dark sorceress and her EVIL spies
is enough to give anyone the shivers. It was
all a bit of a shock to Ethan, I could see that. But
if I'd have reacted like this when I first saw a car,
I'd still be glued to the spot on Camden High
Street.

'In the name of the good goblin, Ethan, will
you just take the bike.'

'But—' Ethan pointed a shaky finger at the
magpie tree.

'Yes, Ethan, we've been through this. The tree talks. Get over it.'

'But it's not possible.'

'Clearly it is.' I let go of the handlebars so Ethan had no choice but to grab his bike.

'This really isn't a game, is it?'

'No, Ethan.' I touched his shoulder. 'But it's going to be OK, I promise.'

Finally Ethan climbed back on his bike and we rode on, Doreen running ahead, her breath rising up into the forest like tiny will-o'-the-wisps. Even she seemed a bit nervous. I mean, it was like totally weird. The forest was deserted – the only noise the swish of our bike wheels and Doreen grunting.

That is why I absolutely could not stop for a wee. I mean, everyone knows the forest grows silent when something really bad is about to happen. I gripped my handlebars tightly and tried to take my mind off the pain in my tummy by counting to a thousand. By the time I got to seven hundred and sixty-four, I could hold it no longer. It was wee or wet myself.

'Wait there a mo,' I said, throwing my bike to the ground. 'Whatever you do, don't follow me.'

'Where are you going?'

'Nowhere you need to come.' I pulled off my rucksack and ran behind a giant oak tree. *A princess is not expected to wee al fresco*, and with Ethan about I wasn't exactly thrilled with the prospect of whipping my trousers down, but when a girl's got to go a girl's got to go. And I really, really had to go.

Just as I began the deed, I heard a rustling noise. It was coming from right in front of me. Slowly I leant sideways and peeped around the tree. Ethan and Doreen were where I'd left them, Ethan's head darting from side to side nervously. It must have been a rabbit or a badger that made the noise. Go away, fluffball, nothing to see here. I fastened my jeans and edged my way around the humongous trunk, my feet sinking into the thick layer of soggy leaves that covered the roots. The wind had picked up, and the knotted branches moaned in the breeze.

More rustling. Behind me this time.

Doreen threw her head back and bleated. She kicked the ground with her heel.

'What's up with her?' Ethan said in a low whisper.

And then I saw it. A grey warty face peeping out from the blanket of leaves. The creature sank back into the ground. It appeared again, closer this time, along with a second face so ugly it could turn unicorn milk sour. I coughed, the stink of sweaty socks and mouldy cheese taking my breath away. There was only one thing that smelt like that.

Boggarts!

The boggarts looked at each other and squealed. One of them had huge yellow teeth that were too big for his mouth.

'Get the helmety-hat,' he said, reaching up out of his hole and grabbing my ankle.

I cried out as the second boggart grabbed me too, his filthy nails jabbing my skin.

'Do something, Ethan,' I shouted.

But Ethan just stood there staring. Nothing new there, then.

'Doreen!'

Doreen ignored me too, her eyes wide, nostrils flared.

'Come on, Do-Do. Help me out.'

'Test is for the highness,' cackled the boggart with big teeth.

*Like, what?*

The other boggarts found this hilarious – their squealing was worse than the Godfather's German techno music. Was it possible to die from bleeding ears? I searched around for something to fight them off with.

A shaft of light broke through the clouds. There was something shiny just in front of me. My bike pump! The boggarts still clinging to my trousers, still squealing, I leant forward and picked it up. A surge of electricity shot up my arm. Weird – but, with the boggarts doing their best to pierce my eardrums, I didn't exactly have time to think about it. I looked right at the nearest screechmonger and, throwing my arm back, whacked him on top of his head.

'Back off, loser,' I shouted.

He yelped and, releasing my leg, shot back down into his hole.

The second boggart – the one who needed a dentist – dug his bony fingers further into my ankle. 'I want me that 'at.'

I kicked him ninja-style right on the nose with my free foot. He cried out and put his hands to his face. For a moment, I felt bad, but then I remembered the throbbing in my leg. It was me or them and it wasn't going to be me. I turned on my heel and prepared to run, but the ground shifted underneath me. I was sinking, dropping down into the earth as the leaves moved in waves around me. Another head appeared, bald with a scaly scalp. Oh my giddy goblin, I wasn't sinking at all. The boggarts were rising!

# CHAPTER 31

There were loads of them now. Faces as ugly as the castle gargoyles, all staring out at me from the leaves. They used their short stubby arms to push themselves upwards, squealing like truffle boars on market day. *Eugh, disgusting.* They smelt even worse than they sounded – had these losers even heard of soap? I covered my nose with my hand.

The boggarts took their chance. One of them climbed out of his hole and butted me in the stomach, sending me flying backwards. Another jumped on top of me. He wrapped his stumpy legs around my neck and pulled at my helmet. I tried to wriggle free, but for a short squat house sprite he was pretty strong. And he had friends – lots of them. Which was more than I had, with both Ethan and Doreen standing there like a pair of bookends. I was boggart fodder for sure . . .

My ears, my ears. How was that sound even possible? The screeching boggart released his grip.

'Get off her!' Ethan squeezed his water bottle again and, still screeching, the boggart backed away, frantically wiping water from his skin. *That explained the smell then!*

I eased myself upwards. 'Stop him, Ethan.'

Old scaly scalp was trying to steal my bike pump – I'd dropped it on the ground when they ambushed me. Ethan held up his bottle and the boggart paused. He gnashed his teeth together, taking another lunge at the pump when Ethan squeezed the bottle and nothing came out.

Nice try, but I was faster than that stink monster. On my feet now, I reached for the pump and charged at him with it. He ran away, crying like a kitten who'd lost its mum. But that didn't stop the other boggarts from having a go.

'No chance,' I said, bringing my bike pump down on top of a bald warty head.

I raised it again. *Bip! Bop! Bosh!* I hit down again and again on one oversized skull after the other. This went on for a while. Ethan gave up on his empty water bottle and joined in with a stumpy stick he'd found. Breathing in short sharp rasps, he whacked the boggarts square on the head like he'd done on the video clip where he was playing whack-a-mole with his dad.

It was totally exhausting. No matter how quickly we went, the boggarts were quicker and another head would appear. Thankfully, the boggarts were getting tired too. Even with their thick skulls there were only so many whacks on the head they could take.

'Truce!' called a particularly ugly boggart with a nose like a squashed aubergine.

I lowered my bike pump but not my guard. The boggart climbed out of his hole. Arms stretched out in front of him, he walked around in a circle. Another joined him. And another. Round and round they went, mouths open, banging into each other like tiny toddler zombies.

*Growling griffins!* Like, how could I have been scared of these dweebs? There was something really strange about this situation. Doreen thought the same. She snapped out of the weird trance thing and shook herself. Bleating manically, she circled the boggarts, gnashing her teeth.

'Stop it, Doreen.' I held out a chocolate lime to tempt her back to me. 'We don't have time for this.'

Doreen continued to chase the zombie-boggarts. She butted old yellow-teeth's bum. For the first time since the magpie tree, a smile crept on to Ethan's face.

'I mean it, Doreen, stop messing—'

My words caught in my throat. One of the boggarts was wearing a cap. A blue-and-white striped bed cap with the royal crest embroidered on it! I ran over and pulled it from his head.

'Where did you get this?'

The boggart snarled. I raised my bike pump and he pressed his hands together like he was about to say his prayers.

'Sorry, missy,' he hissed. 'Please don't 'it me again. The 'lectrics 'urts.'

*Electrics? What was he on about?*

'Where did you get it?' I repeated. 'It's my brother's!'

The boggart closed his eyes. 'I founded it . . .'

'Don't lie to me!' I stuck my bike pump under his chin.

'T'was a gift. A gift from the Lady Odette.'

My stomach tightened. Until now, I'd kind of hoped there'd been a big mix-up and Bertie would just turn up somewhere in the castle with his travel chess set, Jeb following at his heels. But there was no mix-up. Odette *had* kidnapped my brother and dog. It was time to stop stalling and find them.

# CHAPTER 32

I screwed up my eyes, the bright sunshine making them water, and screeched to a stop. We'd made it through the forest but there was no time to rest. The more I'd seen of Odette's silly games, the more worried I was about Bertie and Jeb. 'Here, Doreen,' I called, wrinkling my nose. It smelt like someone had lit a bonfire.

Like, oh my curly candy, major shock or what! Doreen actually did as she was told for once. She stopped nibbling Ethan's shoelace and trotted over. I picked her up and put her in my rucksack. I wasn't taking any chances. Not around Raspberry Ravine – the deep canyon that separated the forest from the cornfields.

'That's some drop,' Ethan said. 'Whoa, what are those big black things?'

'River griffins.'

'What?'

'Don't worry, they're harmless.' *Unless they haven't eaten for a while.* 'Come on.'

Ethan stared at the griffins that were nesting on a ledge on the other side of the narrow ravine. 'Are you sure? They look like pumas with wings.'

'I mean it, Ethan, hurry up!'

He shook his head and followed me along the path that trailed the curve of the gorge to the bridge.

'*No!*' I threw my bike to the ground and stared at the scorched beams where the crossing should have been. Papery cinders flittered in the breeze around me. *So near, yet so far.* I looked longingly across the canyon.

'It's still warm,' Ethan said, running his fingers

over the blackened wood. 'Is this the only crossing?'

'The only one anywhere near the cornfields.'

Doreen bleated and kicked at the inside of my rucksack.

'I know, Do-Do,' I said. 'This is so not good.' In fact it was about as peachy as finding a toenail in your custard. There *was* another bridge to the north, but I had no idea how long it would take to get there. Maybe, if Dad had let me join the Scouts, I might have been able to work it out. But *a princess is not expected to traipse around in the forest.*

I picked up a stone and cupped it in my hand. Edging closer to the ravine, I dropped it over the side. It rocketed towards the ground, disappearing from view long before it hit the bottom. There was like no chance of scrambling down there. I shaded my eyes with my hands and looked over to the other side of the ravine. 'We're going to have to jump it.'

'You're joking, right? You'd have to be off your rocker.'

I rolled my eyes. Sure, it was risky. The ravine was so high even the griffins had altitude sickness, but it was narrow, and ever since my major fail in the bowl, I'd been working hard on catching air. OK, I hadn't completely cracked it yet, but I stayed on my bike most of the time, and I've always been better under pressure.

'It's not that far, admittedly.' Ethan crouched down and rubbed the scorched ground. 'But it's all in the run-up, you see.'

The wind whistled, sending a cloud of dust towards me. There was a sickly smell in the air. Beyond the caves, on the other side of the ravine, I saw a purple cloud. There was only one thing that made a sherbet cloud like that, a sherbet dragon. So, Tufty was right about Alun being at the cornfields, and the ruined bridge suggested he was probably right about Odette too.

'Sorry, Do-Do,' I said, fastening the lid of my bag. 'But this is our best shot at finding Bertie.'

'And there's no room for error here,' Ethan continued. 'I mean, come on, if you fall you die.'

I climbed on my bike and rode back to the edge of the trees. 'Best not fall then.'

Speed, it was all about speed. That's what Ethan had said when we were practising in the park. Keep your bike straight, look ahead, and shred like your life depends on it. I never thought my life *would* depend on it.

I took a deep breath and, eyes fixed on the caves opposite, rode towards the black slit of the ravine. Just before I hit the edge, I stopped pedalling and stood up straight. Holding my pedals level, I pulled back on my handlebars and shifted my weight forward then back. My bike lifted off the ground, and I flew through the air towards the opposite bank.

I hit the ground with a heavy thud. My wheel slipped and I fell sideways. Winded, I lay there on the cold ground, pain shooting up my hip, but then I remembered Doreen. *No!* I pushed myself up on to my knees and, ignoring the blood dripping from my elbow, pulled my rucksack off. My hands shook as I undid the lid – why wasn't she moving? Forcing back tears, I opened my bag.

A pointy ear twitched.

Brown eyes stared up at me from under long lashes.

And a purple tongue tickled my hand.

Thank the good goblin – she was OK!

I lifted Doreen out of the bag and hugged her tight. On the other side of the ravine Ethan was about to jump. I knew he'd follow me. He was

too competitive not to, even if there was a chance he'd plunge to his death and be eaten by river griffins.

But the river griffins were going to have to look elsewhere for a meal today. Ethan made the most awesome jump ever, landing without even a wobble.

'Now quit with the faffing,' I said as we bumped fists. 'We've a prince to save.'

# CHAPTER 33

Spooktastic or what. I'd never been to the cornfields and right now, I figured I never wanted to go there again. It was the creepiest place ever. The giant maize danced in the wind, like it was alive, its rustling making the bad feeling in my tummy even worse.

'What the womble—' Ethan pointed at the sooty path that cut the field in two.

My throat closed. A perfectly straight line of charred stubble, it was so neat and even it had to have been made by magic. I followed it anyway,

Ethan muttering nervously to himself, Doreen trailing a few paces behind, her nostrils flaring.

The path led to a scorched clearing. I grabbed Doreen's teddy-bear pyjama top and stopped. The smell of burnt earth made my nose tingle. But there was something else in the air too? Something sweet. Sherbet.

Sure enough, Alun was on the other side of the clearing. He bellowed and a cloud of purple dust rose from his nostrils. He was every bit as magnificent as the pictures I'd seen in Bertie's natural history book.

Ethan grabbed my arm. 'Tell me that's not real.'

'Chill, Ethan. It's just Alun.'

'Alun.'

'Yes, Alun. Hush, you'll scare him.'

'*Scare him?* Have you lost it altogether?'

'It's fine, Ethan – so long as his sherbet hasn't gone bad.'

Then things could get a little more interesting – if you consider melting flesh and boiling blood to be interesting. Why had my EVIL auntie brought him here? Was this another one of her games?

Alun snorted again, louder this time. I took a step forward and stopped. There was a definite fizz in the air. The alarm bells were ringing big-style.

'Ava? Are you OK?'

I nodded and handed Ethan my rucksack. 'Stay here and keep an eye on Doreen.'

While death by sherbet was not high on my agenda, sometimes you have to ignore the alarm bells ringing in your head and do what your heart tells you. And despite everything, my heart told me to go to Alun.

The dragon seemed bigger up close. He was taller than one of the red London buses. The purple scales on his long, thick neck shimmered like the inside of a shell. He looked up at the sky and started to shake. I backed away. I really hoped my heart was right because my head was telling me I was toast.

'Shush, Alun,' I said. 'You have to stay calm.'

Alun scratched the floor, his talons leaving lines in the dust. Poor thing – I could see now that his other foot was tied to a hex chain, binding him to the spot. It had dug deep, bloody lines in his ankle. No wonder he was panicking.

'It's OK,' I said softly. 'I want to help.' I showed him my palms. 'See, I'm not going to hurt you.'

Alun stretched his long neck towards me. He looked at me quizzically.

'You can trust me, Alun. I promise.'

I took a deep breath and, crouching down next to his humongous foot, loosened the chain.

A shadow fell across the cornfields, the sun dwarfed by a single black cloud. The cloud billowed angrily, its centre twisting and swirling like a tornado. Beyond the cloud there was a single trail of purple-tinged vapour. The chain around Alun's foot sizzled, scorching my fingers, and turned to dust.

Alun threw his head back, his nostrils flaring. I curled my hands into tight fists.

'Calm, boy,' I said. *Please don't let him snort sherbet.*

Alun watched the vapour trail. He was shaking like a giant scaly jelly, but somehow he controlled his sherbet. The trail now a smudge in the distance, he grew calmer. He sighed and looked at me with warm, trusting eyes.

I reached up and patted him. 'See, it's all going to be OK.'

Alun didn't look too sure. He nudged me with his muzzle and stepped to the side.

That's when I saw it. The freaky pumpkin head in the corn behind him. It stared down at me with black triangle eyes, its mouth carved into a scream.

The pumpkin head belonged to a bedraggled scarecrow. The wind pulled on its smock making it look like it was moving. I stepped towards it, tripping over Doreen, who pushed past me and charged towards the pole. So much for Ethan keeping an eye on her.

'No, Doreen,' I shouted, trying to grab her mane.

She bucked and ran around in circles under the scarecrow, bleating like a goat who'd just realized its owners were not vegetarian.

'Calm down, Doreen.'

Doreen butted me in the kneecap. Like she hadn't tested her skull enough today, she jumped up at the scarecrow and butted the pole.

*Like, what!*

I covered my mouth with my hand. That's what she'd been trying to tell me – the scarecrow was wearing Bertie's shoes. How could I have missed those black-and-white tiger-striped loafers?

Doreen jumped up at the pole again.

The scarecrow turned its head.

It stared at me with its black triangle eyes.

'Avariella,' it said. 'Stop messing around with Doreen and untie me right now.'

# CHAPTER 34

Oh yes, the pumpkin-headed scarecrow was Bertie, all right. He was firing instructions like arrows. *Stop messing around with Doreen.* I mean, he had to be kidding, right? How about a thank-you for risking life, limb and Dad's finger wag to come and rescue him?

Bertie rolled his shoulders and stretched his arms out. 'Thank goodness for that. I thought you were never going to get me down. I'm as stiff as a newly starched apron.'

Being tied to a pole for griffin knows how long

had clearly not made my brother any less annoying. Still, I suppose I should be grateful he was OK. I just wished I knew Jeb was OK too, but Bertie said he had no idea where Odette had taken him. 'Here, let me help you.' I cupped my hands under Bertie's chin and wriggled the pumpkin from side to side. 'Are you sure you can't think of anything that might help us find Jeb?'

'Ouch! What in the name of Biscotti do you think you are doing?'

'I'm trying to get this stupid thing off your head.' It really was a snug fit.

'I beg your pardon?'

*Like, what?* This wasn't good. 'Erg, nothing—'

'Nothing – you look like you've seen a ghost.'

If only. What I was seeing was far scarier.

Bertie swatted a mayfly away from his cheek. 'Oh my word,' he said, running his fingers over his orange fleshy face. 'No wonder I have tunnel vision.'

Oh my word indeed. Watch out, gingerbread boy, because there was a new contender for the tastiest child in Biscotti. My brother was part-boy part-pumpkin.

'Well, let's not dwell on the matter.' Bertie pulled off the sack trousers he'd been dressed in. 'I'm sure there's a fix for this predicament. Our priority now must be to find Sir Jeffrey and return home.'

Ethan stared at Bertie, his eyebrows furrowed. The short rest Bertie had requested *in order that he might recombobulate* had failed to recombobulate Ethan.

'I'm terribly sorry.' Bertie offered Ethan his hand. 'It would appear my sister has forgotten her manners. His Royal Highness Prince Bertrand Cornelius Victor Custardo D'Alessandro of Biscotti, at your service.'

'But you can call him Bertie,' I said.

Ethan continued to stare.

Bertie turned his pumpkin-head towards me. 'Is he OK? He seems a bit out of sorts.'

'He's fine, Bertie. I'll explain later. Now put your trousers back on and let's get out of here.'

'I will not.' Bertie's triangle eyes grew narrow. 'Have you felt how rough the fabric is? It could cause some serious chafing.' He took off his smock and straightened his favourite blue-and-white-striped nightshirt, waving to Alun who started to pant like an excited dog.

'Well, I hope you're wearing underpants, Bertie, because that nightshirt is way too short. Come on, you too, Ethan. We need to get out of here.'

I scanned the cornfields, my heart sinking like a duck who'd eaten leaden bread. How in the Other World were we ever going to find Jeb? I knew this had all been too easy.

'Keep your witchy-wig on.' Bertie pulled the sack trousers from Doreen's teeth. 'We're coming, aren't we, Do-Do? So, what's the plan?'

'Plan is we get out of here fast.'

'But I protest. A knight doesn't go into battle without a strategy.'

Ethan moved closer to Bertie. 'Actually, Ava, a plan would be kind of nice right now.'

*No kidding.* Alun had been my only clue. I had

no idea where to start looking for Jeb.

'Do you remember anything about how you got here, Bertie?' I asked. 'Maybe Jeb ran off somewhere on the way?'

'I'm afraid I don't. This whole experience has been most perplexing. What I do recall is hearing a noise and slipping on my favourite loafers to investigate. Next thing I was being tied to a pole by a pretty lady with the most appalling onion breath.'

The corn danced in the wind behind us, the air heavy with soot and dust. Bertie put his hand to his orange fleshy mouth and coughed. 'Well, if you don't have a plan, Avariella, did you at least manage to bring refreshments? My throat feels like sandpaper.'

'Sorry, Bertie, I didn't exactly have time to pack a picnic.'

Bertie looked at Ethan with his hands on his hips. 'Honestly, what I wouldn't give for a nice cup of Earl Grey.'

In the name of the good goblin, that was it. The tea leaves. What if Aunt Maude's reading was further into the future? Maybe she wasn't wrong about seeing Bertie and Jeb at the Limonadi River. Maybe they just hadn't both got there yet? It was a long shot, but it was the only shot we had.

'Let's go – quick – I think I know where Jeb is. By the Limonadi River!'

'And where did this sudden revelation come from?'

'Just come on, Bertie. Grab Doreen – I'll explain on the way.' I ran around Alun towards the bikes.

'Wait, Avariella.' Bertie patted Alun, who wagged his tail, corn crashing to the ground. 'Calm down, boy. You'll take us all out with that thing.'

'Bertie, be careful. His sherbet!'

'Oh, balderdash. If he hasn't excreted sulphuric crystals by now it's not going to happen.' He stroked Alun's leg and the dragon lay down, curling his tail like a spiral staircase. 'Not after what we've been through together, hey, Alun?'

Alun bent his neck and licked the stubby stalk on top of Bertie's head.

'Now what have I told you. I'm not much of a cuddler.'

Was this for real? Bertie had now stepped on to Alun's tail.

'Come along, you two,' he said. 'Alun will have us there in no time. The dragon and I have become quite good friends over the course of our captivity. Though I must say, he's a bit affection-ate for my liking.'

Ethan made a weird splurting noise somewhere between a cough and a cry. 'He is kidding, right?'

'It's OK. Bertie's right, Alun's not going to hurt us.'

Ethan flashed me his palms and backed away.

'Oh, for goblin's sake.' Even with a round orange head Bertie still managed to look snooty. 'Have you no spine, boy?'

'What?' Ethan glared at Bertie.

'He's calling you a wimp.'

'That I am. Now come on. Take the coward's route if you will, but I think Sir Jeffrey would prefer us to take the dragon express.'

# CHAPTER 35

The dragon express it was then. Bertie made his way along Alun's tail, his nightshirt riding up in a very disturbing manner as he lost his footing and leant forward to correct his balance. He pulled it down and continued up the dragon's back, using the raised scales that ran along his spine for footholds. Plopping himself down, he placed a leg either side of Alun's neck, and called down to Ethan.

'See, easy as algebra.'

Ethan shook his head. Smiling nervously, he

climbed up Alun's back and nestled down behind Bertie in the dip between the dragon's shoulders. Doreen secured safely in my rucksack, I followed, slipping into position behind Ethan where I could make sure he was OK. *Dragon-riding, like wow!* If I wasn't so worried about Jeb, I'd have been whooping with excitement.

'We're ready, Alun, if we may,' said Bertie. 'The bicycles, please.'

Alun used his teeth to pick up the rope we'd tied our bikes together with.

'See,' said Bertie. 'What the dragon lacks in courage, he makes up for in intelligence.'

Bertie was right. Alun was a total wuss, but he wasn't short on brain power. The BMXs dangling from his mouth like a mouse caught by the tail, the dragon shifted his weight forward and tensed. Glancing over his shoulder, he unfolded his wings, the purple skin as thin as paper, and thrust upwards. Like, oh my giddy goblin, we were flying.

Upwards we soared into the wind, my hair whipping around my face and my stomach leapfrogging.

'Sick!' Ethan's voice wavered in the breeze. 'This is one way to catch big air.'

*Was it!* Sack-racing was now down to number three on my list of favourite things to do, BMX coming in first, closely followed by dragon-riding.

'It is jolly exciting,' Bertie said. 'Though I wish my nightshirt would stop blowing up.'

Skimming the edge of the forest, we followed the curve of the ravine. The cornfields on our right, to our left the thick canopy of the Black Forest. I leant to the side, searching for a gap between the trees, desperate to catch a glimpse of the knights. Where were they? Even on foot they should have made it through by now.

'There, Alun.' Bertie pointed to the gleaming Limonadi River. 'Can you see it? I told you it wasn't far.'

Alun snorted and began his descent. In the distance I caught sight of the Doughnut Hills and the lush green plains that now lined the north-eastern side of the ravine. The Limonadi River meandered below, cutting the plains in two, the magnificent golden boulders along its western bank glimmering in the sun like giant polished cannonballs.

'Fool's gold,' said Bertie. 'An ill omen, indeed.'

Alun landed in the grass just beyond the second river crossing. It was the kind of grass that tasted milky when you chewed it and made you want to take your shoes off. But I don't think that was why Alun didn't want to go beyond it. In fact, I'm certain of it. But I had no choice but to make my way towards the river. I had to find Jeb. I pushed away the doubt and slid down Alun's back.

'Thank you, Alun,' I said, tipping Doreen out of my rucksack. 'Ethan, untie the bikes. I'll go ahead and make sure it's safe.'

Electricity crackled in the air and a fork of purple lightning split the sky in two. In the distance I heard a frightened bark. *Jeb!* Ignoring Alun's high-pitched warning, I ran towards my puppy.

# CHAPTER 36

It hit me first in the shoulder. Then the chest. The second lightning bolt so powerful I flew into the air and landed on my back near the edge of the riverbank. What had just happened? It was like being struck with a supercharged lance. I rolled over on to my knees and pushed myself up. The lance struck again. This was it! The ride was over for Ava.

Laughter, tinkling like unicorn bells.

Pain in my head so bad I thought my brain was going to explode.

And then a voice – strong and firm – *you'll never win, Avariella*...

Followed by a final blow that sent me stumbling backwards into the river.

Gasping at the shock of the icy water, I kicked my legs like a cane toad with a sugar rush, trying to stay afloat. But there was something pulling me down.

'Help,' I shouted, forcing my head back above the surface and spitting out a mouth full of sweet fizzy water. 'Ethan, Bertie – please!'

The pull grew stronger.

Too strong to fight.

The darkness swallowed me.

I lifted my arms above my head, hands cupped, scooping the churning water as fast as I could. But it was no use – I couldn't break through the surface. The river surged and I was spinning. Slowly at first, gradually picking up speed until I was whirling faster than a whipping top. Rocketing towards the riverbed, I let out a silent scream. No river could be this deep – it had to be enchanted.

The spinning stopped. The water was warm now. I felt calm, sleepy. Maybe I was dreaming because I was somehow floating above my body. I stared down at my white waxy face, an air bubble rising from my nostril. Memories flashed before me, flickering like the old television set in Kaye's café: cuddling up with Aunt Maude reading stories; my seventh birthday party when Mum got annoyed because I threw up in the chocolate fountain; sliding down the stairs in a potato sack with Bertie timing me . . .

*Bertie!* He might be a dweeb but he was my brother. What if the lance was now turned on him and Ethan? I had to make sure they were OK.

Light shone above and everything went fuzzy. I felt a pull like I was being snatched upwards by a giant magnet, and somehow I was back inside my body. Fingers pointed, I lifted my arms above my head and swam, dragging myself up through the water. I had to get to Bertie.

The quicker I swam, the less dreamy I felt. There was a burning energy inside me as though the lightning bolt had supercharged my muscles. My arms cut through the water so fast my legs could just keep up. Sunlight shone above, sending dappled beams towards me. The surface rippled and my hands broke through. Gasping for air, I dragged myself on to the riverbank, snorting snot and water. Chest burning, I coughed up shedloads more water and rolled over on to my back. I shut my eyes and tried to slow my breathing. I just needed a minute to rest. Then I'd find Bertie and Ethan.

'Oh, Ava . . .'

I felt a prod in my neck. I tilted my head and prised open my eyes. Gucci boots! I sat up, water dripping from my hair on to the shiny leather.

'Ava, Ava, Ava.' Odette took a hanky out of her pocket and wiped the toe of her boot. 'I told you our cycle paths would cross again. How have you enjoyed my little challenges? I have to say, I'm most impressed with your resilience. Bravo.'

I clambered to my feet. 'What have you done with Bertie and Ethan?'

My EVIL auntie nodded downstream to

where the river dropped into a gentle waterfall surrounded by rock pools. Ethan and Bertie were sitting with their feet in the biggest pool, Ethan's jeans soaked up to his knees, the BMXs on the floor next to him. There was a giant bubble around them, it shimmered in the sunshine. My heart leapt like an Apollonian mountain frog. Jeb was in the bubble too, splashing around in one of the pools.

'Jeb!'

'He can't hear you. They're in their own little rock-pool world, hunting for unicorn fish. *Idiots!*'

Talking of unicorns, where was Doreen? I couldn't see her anywhere. Alun had disappeared too, which wasn't that much of a surprise given he'd refused to come anywhere near the river-bank.

'Fancy bringing your little boyfriend along.' Odette laughed. 'Daddy would not be happy with you fraternizing with the peasants.'

'He's not my boyfriend! Why does everyone keep calling him my boyfriend?'

'No matter. He has to die. Your brother too. I refuse to have three children trailing along with me. I know big families are fashionable in the Home Counties, but it's just not my designer bag!'

# CHAPTER 37

I edged backwards, the Limonadi River burbling behind me. So that was Odette's plan – for me and her to go off and play happy families? *Unlikely.* And what was with the killing everyone? Like no need! It was clear, my auntie wasn't just EVIL. She was SUPER-EVIL.

'You are kidding, right? You can't just go around killing children because they don't fit with your plans.' I glanced back over to the rock-pool bubble. 'And no way am I coming with you, whatever you have in mind.'

Odette's perfect smile faded for a second, but only a second. 'Never mind, I know it's a big change for you having a new mummy. That's why I brought your little doggy along. I hope he gets on with Elvis. I'm afraid poor 'Vis is in the doggy hospital at the moment. Had a bit of a run-in with a stiletto heel.' She jabbed me in the chest, a spark of electricity firing from her red painted nail, and chuckled to herself. 'Still, who needs two eyes anyway?'

I took another step back, careful not to edge too close to the water.

'Oh, sorry, darling. Was that a bit sharp? It's just I'm so excited. Finally, we can be together. You must have felt it, Ava. It's you I wanted all along.'

*Maybe I should swim for it?* I was excellent at holding my breath – I practised in the bath all the time. But even if I could escape Odette, what would she do to Ethan and Bertie?

'I only took your brother to test you,' she continued. 'To see whether it was worth investing. Well, I'm delighted to inform you, you've passed. Tut, tut, disobeying Daddy like that.'

Odette wagged her finger just like Dad. It was the scariest thing I'd seen all day.

'And so brave and intuitive. The sprites predicted you'd fail at the boggarts, or they'd at least see a little gore at the ravine. But I never doubted you. I know what runs through your veins.'

I stood up straight, head held high. I was feeling stronger now. Hands on hips, I squared up to Odette. She seemed to enjoy this, standing so close I could see the pulse in her neck. Bertie was right – she really did have onion breath. 'Well, let my brother go then!' I said. 'He's served his purpose.'

Odette clapped her hands together. 'That's my girl. Such spirit! But you'll have to try harder than that to convince me. I have a reputation to build. One can't terrify the people without doing terrifying things.'

She clicked her fingers and Bertie jumped up from his rock-pool seat, the bubble evaporating instantly. His eyes fixed on Odette, he walked towards us. Ethan stayed where he was, staring into the rock pool with Jeb.

'The charms hit them a little stronger than I intended, what with them being from the Other World and all. Your boyfriend will come round soon enough. Right in time for you to help me annihilate him.'

'Oh my curly candy, you're as mad as a box of cauldron frogs.'

'Now, darling, please stop. There really is no point fighting it. Us baddies have to stick together. I have great plans for us. I'm thinking we start with taking over Biscotti, go get our nails done and then move on to the Other World.'

I shivered. The first sun was going down, casting a pink haze over the river. My wet clothes clung to me. Odette offered me her cashmere cape. I gave her my best dirty look.

'Well, maybe we'll leave the Other World domination for now,' she laughed. 'And concentrate on Biscotti. I have my developers working on the blueprints as we speak. Imagine it, Ava, the biggest theme park ever. It's inspired –

real-life Disney Kingdom meets the Tower of London. The Other World folk are just mad for magic and unicorns. Throw in the odd dragon and a few old relics and they'll be lining up to visit. It will annoy your dad so much. Especially when he finds out he's one of the exhibits.'

'You wouldn't.'

How could she even think of doing such a thing? Beautiful, magical Biscotti turned into a zoo for the Other World folk and Dad one of the main attractions? *No!* The Kingdom would be changed for ever, and not in a good way. In time, the magic of Biscotti would surely die, just like it had died in the Other World.

'I most certainly would. Don't tell me you wouldn't be happier rid of your father and all his rules. We're not like the rest of the family – blooming goody-goodies – we're free spirits. That's why my brother hates us so.'

'Hates me?' I felt like someone was sitting on my chest. Dad didn't hate me, did he? Sometimes, when he sighed at my games or had a go at me for nothing, it felt like he did. I mean, he never shouted at Bertie – not like he shouted at me.

I stared at my brother, who had made his way over from the rock pool. It was hard to tell what he was thinking with those black triangle eyes, but the fact he wouldn't look at me made my tummy churn.

Odette did a fake yawn. 'All that silly business about what a princess is and isn't expected to do! It's just so tiring.'

I got a horrible taste in my mouth. How many times had I thought that?

'Girls like you and me – modern girls – we know what we want and we get it. And I want my kingdom back! I'm the rightful heir.'

Odette's hair crackled with electricity. She fired a lightning bolt into the pink haze. I swallowed back the gobstopper-sized lump in my throat. But I was more frightened by her words than her sorcery. Seriously, I was going to puke. What she'd said, well, it was all kind of true . . .

Except Odette had given away her right to the kingdom when she turned EVIL!

'Just think what we could achieve together,' she said, bouncing on the balls of her feet. 'You and me best friends for ever, just like things were with Aunt Maude before I fried her brain.'

*What!* A bead of sweat trickled down my forehead. So that was the *something* nobody ever talked about. How could anyone hurt Maude?

'We're the same, you and me, Ava. The same.'

'Bertie?'

My skin prickled. He was backing away, holding his hand over his jaggered pumpkin mouth. I had to put a stop to Odette's silly games right now. I might not be the perfect princess, but I was not the same as my EVIL auntie.

'No.' I was surprised by how calm I sounded because my heart was beating against my ribs like a caged pixie. 'I'm nothing like you. You're EVIL and I hate you!'

The sky grew dark and Odette's hair went all weird and floaty, her eyes perfect black circles as she stared into nothing. Bertie whimpered. I needed to do something fast. *Think, Ava, think.*

I thought about it for as long as I could, which

given I was about to be annihilated by my EVIL auntie was like a nanosecond. But that was OK. Because what was there to think about? I mean, there's only one thing you can do when your EVIL auntie wants to kill you.

'Leg it!'

# CHAPTER 38

*W*ow! My EVIL auntie really was laying it on with the Black Sorceress thing. She had her eyes closed, her arms pointing upwards in a V-shape, and was humming like a motorbike. Fear bubbled in my stomach. You didn't need to be a detective to work out she was leading up to something big.

I grabbed Bertie's arm. 'Come on, run!'

Odette's eyes flickered open. *Oops, I didn't mean to shout.* She cracked her knuckles and pointed her finger at me. 'Have it your way then.'

I ducked, only narrowly avoiding the purple lightning bolt, which hit the river and bounced across the surface of the water.

'Bertie, get out of here, now!'

Odette yawned. Rolling her shoulders, she reached up, her fingers spread. The air crackled with electricity, a fork of lightning splitting the sky in two. I covered my eyes to protect them from the glare of Odette's ring. Oh my giddy goblin, she was harvesting the lightning.

'Go, Bertie!'

There was no way I could fight her but maybe I could distract my EVIL auntie while the others escaped. Hide in the boulders perhaps—

From behind the giant rocks shot a white shape – Doreen must have had the hide-in-the-boulders idea earlier! She flew into the air like a cannonball and butted Odette in the stomach. Mouth open, my EVIL auntie tottered backwards and landed on her bum, Doreen landing on top of her, kicking and gnashing her teeth. *Way to go, Do-Do!*

'Get this stinking thing off me,' Odette

screamed. 'Do you have any idea how much these trousers cost?' She picked Doreen up and chucked her sideways.

Doreen bleated like she'd never bleated before, and charged at Odette again. It was time to get Bertie to safety. What did he think he was doing, just standing there by the rock pools with his great big pumpkin head? And where was Ethan? His bike had gone – surely he wouldn't have just abandoned us? I legged it over to Bertie and picked up my BMX.

'Quick, sit on the handlebars.'

'I will not. How undignified.'

'Just do it—'

I put my hands to my ears – the scream would have curdled blood.

'No!'

Doreen was hovering in the air, level with Odette's head, a luminous purple light surrounding her like an all-body halo. She stared right at me, her eyes round and wild. Screaming again, she tensed – and turned to stone, one of her legs snapping off as she thudded to the ground.

I wanted to crumple to the floor too – my poor Do-Do – but I had to stay strong for Bertie. He had turned whiter than a newborn unicorn.

'Games over.' Odette kicked Doreen's broken-off leg out of the way and clicked her fingers. A diamond-encrusted broomstick flew towards her. 'It's time to get radical, as I believe you BMXers like to say.'

Quivering, Bertie picked up Jeb who was covering his eyes with his paws and stuck him inside the top of his nightshirt. He tried to climb on to my handlebars, but agility was never one of Bertie's strong points and the EVIL sorceress hovering above our heads was a bit of a distraction.

'It really didn't have to be like this, Avariella.' Odette made a grab for Bertie.

I reached for his nightshirt, but I was too late. She already had him. She waved him above me, her long thin fingers wrapped around his wrist. I was scared to look up – he never did say if he had underpants on.

'You are bold, my darling, but foolish.'

I stretched upwards towards Bertie. Poor Jeb was holding on to the collar of my brother's nightshirt with his teeth.

'Do something, Ava!' Bertie shouted.

'Shut it, tubby. I'm talking to your sister.' Bertie cried out as Odette dug her nails into his wrist. 'I'm prepared to give her another chance. After all, it seems such a shame to waste one so spirited.'

I reached up again. This time my fingers scraped the sole of Bertie's shoe. Close, but not close enough.

'Oh, just quit with the evil and let my brother go!'

Odette's laughter tinkled across the vast silent meadow. 'Fine. Have it your way.' She let go of Bertie's wrist and he thudded to the ground.

I felt sick. 'No!' I shouted. 'Nooooo!'

'I mean business, Ava. There's no room for compassion when you're running an evil empire. You'll see that. Even if I have to teach you the hard way.'

Odette pointed her finger at me, sparks flying

from her nail. I prepared myself for the electric lance. But it was Odette who wailed in pain. *Like, what?* Jeb was hanging from her nose, his jaw clamped tight around it. He swung from side to side, growling, trying to avoid her nails as she jabbed at him with one hand and attempted to control the broomstick with the other.

I legged it to Bertie. 'Are you OK?'

Bertie groaned – he gave me the thumbs up and wrapped his arms around his ribs. He seemed OK, and right now I had to concentrate on Odette. Jeb would only be able to distract her for so long. And what then?

A surge of electricity shot up my leg. I touched my sock where my bike pump was glowing. I had zero clue what was going on, but you didn't need to work for Bikes-r-Us to know the blue glow meant this was no ordinary pump. No wonder the Godfather had gone on so much about keeping it safe. I looked up at Odette. Having an electric doodah thing was all very well, but what was I supposed to do with it?

A low rumble travelled through the ground

towards me and my nose tingled. Slowly I turned round. Alun was charging across the meadow with Ethan on his back. Ethan waved. He pointed to Alun, swooshing his arm upwards into the air like an aeroplane taking off.

'Remember, Ava,' he called. 'It's all in the run-up.'

I nodded, a smile creeping into the corners of my mouth. It was time for some extreme whack-a-mole!

# CHAPTER 39

E than and Alun picked up speed, thundering across the grass towards us. And a good thing too. Odette had finally managed to get Jeb off her nose. She shook him and hurled him towards the ground.

'Die, fluffball!'

My stomach did a 360 flip. But Ethan and Alun were on it. Racing past the giant glimmering boulders, the dragon swished his mighty tail, catching Jeb with the tip and flicking him upwards.

'Nice one,' Ethan grabbed hold of Jeb, gripping him like a rugby ball. 'Now, Alun!' he called. 'Sherbet!' Still clutching my quivering puppy, he bounced down Alun's scaly ribs, landing on his feet and legging it towards Bertie.

I crossed my fingers. And my arms. And my eyes. I mean, if Alun got it wrong and squirted the wrong type of sherbet, we'd die. But we had to trust him. Just like he'd trusted us.

Alun let out a mighty snort and the air grew heavy with sweet, sugary powder. A most excellent job! Not a single burning corpse in sight. Coolio – I was ready to take down my EVIL auntie.

Above me Odette was giving it loads with the extreme cursing. I could hear her – I mean, the whole of Biscotti could probably hear her – but I couldn't see her.

And, more importantly, she couldn't see me.

When the sherbet cloud disappeared, I was hiding among the boulders behind Alun with my front wheel pointing at his tail.

Odette, covered in a film of purple dust,

darted from side to side above him. 'I'm coming for you, Ava!'

*Wrong!* I was coming for her. Holding the handlebars steady, I pegged it towards Alun. Eyes fixed on the top of his head, I leant forward then back, keeping my arms and legs straight. My front wheel lifted off the ground and I lowered it on to Alun's tail. He snorted and flattened his scales, my wheels drumming over his bony spine as I shredded up his back. Almost at his head now, I tore my bike pump from my sock. With my other hand, I pulled my handlebars back. Thanking the good goblin for BMX, I flew towards Odette.

*Thwack!* Bang on target. I brought the pump down hard on the top of my EVIL auntie's skull. It flashed, and blue sparks shot from her ears. The sparks spread around her head, her hair alive with fiery blue light, then fizzled out like a spent firework. She opened her mouth, her shiny red lips a perfect circle, and plummeted from her broomstick.

I fell right beside her.

'Ava!' Ethan stepped over Odette's twitching body. 'Are you all right?'

'Yes. I think so.' Jeb jumped out of Ethan's arms. Whimpering, he sniffed my grazed cheek and licked me gently on the nose. I eased myself up to sitting and pulled him close. Burying my face in his soft fur, I squeezed my eyelids together. I wouldn't cry. Not even with relief.

'Gnarly,' Ethan continued. 'I won't lie, you're the most radical princess since Leia.'

*Who?* I stood up.

'It was rather impressive.' Bertie's thick orange skin was damp with sweat. He kept looking at the twitching Odette. 'But you do know Dad's going to kill you when he finds out about that bicycle?'

I pulled him close and hugged him. 'You're OK, then. Come on, let's get out of here.'

Odette had stopped twitching and was now lying perfectly still, her clothes crackling with electricity. But she had magic. We were not safe yet.

Ethan picked up his bike. 'Suits me.'

'Wait! Doreen. Where's Doreen?' Panic rose in my chest at the memory of that bloodcurdling scream.

Bertie picked up my rucksack, straining with the weight of the petrified microcorn. 'I'm afraid she doesn't look well. But you know how unicorns bounce back.'

Doreen did not look like she was bouncing back any time soon. She'd been frozen in motion, her front legs kicking in defence, teeth bared.

'Oh my giddy goblin, no!'

'Be calm, sister. She's a microcorn. She has plenty of lives to spare yet—'

Alun nudged Bertie with his muzzle and looked over at the giant fool's-gold boulders. He licked Bertie's orange cheek and, reeling his neck back in, unfolded his wings and took off.

'Like, thanks, Alun.' I put my hands on my hips and watched him zoom upwards into the sky. A trip through the Black Forest in the dark it was, then.

'Oh, you can't blame him.' Bertie pointed at

the boulders where a shadowy figure had emerged. 'That ridiculous haircut is enough to scare anyone.'

# CHAPTER 40

'L ike, no way.' Ethan grabbed my arm. 'It's a punk riding a unicorn. Where's my phone? I've got to get a selfie with him.'

Like, no way indeed. The unicorn whinnied, her horn glowing in the orange dusky light. She rose up on her back legs, the rider holding on to her mane with one hand and raising the other arm in salute, fist clenched. The sun reflecting off his gold tooth, he smiled.

'What?' Ethan stopped fiddling with his phone. 'I'm not lying – I've seen that punk dude before in the café.'

I'm not lying either. I'd seen the punk too. It made like zero sense, but on the back of the unicorn sat the spiky-headed man. And just in case that wasn't enough to make your brain explode, racing along behind him on a bright pink mountain bike was . . . Mum!

If Mum was shocked by the fact her youngest child was now part-boy part-vegetable, she didn't show it. She threw down her bike and they ran towards each other, Bertie's oversized pumpkin-head wobbling like a bobble-head doll.

'Hurry, Sir Louseylot,' she called. 'We've found them.'

Wowzas, I had no idea Mum could run so fast. Her Other World trainers must have helped. She had jeans on too and her hair was pulled back into a ponytail which she wore low under a base-ball cap. She threw herself at Bertie, smothering him in a tight bear hug. Pausing to blow me a kiss and fuss Jeb, she began to examine his pumpkin head.

The spiky-headed man broke away from the rest of the group and sped towards me and Ethan. He jumped down from the unicorn and straightened his silver tracksuit top. There was a P emblem on the front, just like the one on my bike pump. On the back was written the word 'Surveillance'. He pushed his mirrored sunglasses up.

'All right, princess,' he said. 'Fancy meeting you here.' He turned and held his hand out to Ethan. 'Kevin,' he added. 'Pleased to meet you. Now if you don't mind, where is she? My chakra crystals are going ballistic.'

*Like, what!* Could things get any weirder? He was chuffin' Kevin. Chuffin' Kevin, of the chuffin' chakra crystals. So, that's why he'd been following me.

'Guys?' Kevin sniffed and rubbed his nose.

So much for the surveillance jacket – Odette was just behind us – I mean, did he not have eyes in his head?

Ethan pointed towards my EVIL auntie. But before Kevin could even move, there was a flash of light and we were swallowed by a cloud of luminous purple smoke. The smoke disappeared as quickly as it came . . . and with it went Odette.

'Oh, bother,' Mum said, approaching with Bertie and a bizarrely grey Sir Louseylot. 'That is unfortunate.' She placed an arm around me and kissed my head. 'Thank goodness you're OK.'

'You're not angry—'

'Shush.' Mum put her finger on my lips. 'We have more pressing matters to attend to.' She waved at Ethan like he was an old friend.

Ethan waved back, unsure. His confusion was not helped by the fact Mum was wearing a Foo Fighters T-shirt. *Yes, I know – parents in band T-shirts. Kill me now.*

Ethan wasn't the only one giving out funny looks. Kevin shot Sir Louseylot the evils. 'That's your fault. I told you we didn't have time to stop and say hello to your mum.'

'And I told you, I had to go to the toilet.' Close up Sir Louseylot looked like a statue. Even his clothes were grey and he had a weird sheen like the polished rocks Bertie collected. He edged a leg carefully over the dappled Shire horse he was riding. Holding on to the mane, he paused and stared at the ground.

'Just jump, you wuss.' Kevin tutted and bent down to examine the ground where Odette had disappeared. 'I just don't get it,' he continued. 'Petrification, teleportation: she was always such a rubbish sorceress.'

'Your Other World surveillance has failed again,' said Louseylot primly. 'If anyone is to blame for this mess, it's you.'

Kevin put his sunglasses back on. 'I'm beginning to wish I'd left you frozen in the forest.'

*Leave the petrifying for the knights!* Of course, that's why Louseylot looked like a statue. He'd been turned to stone by those pesky forest sprites. I knew that dude was a rotten egg – it would take more than chocolate blossom to disguise his stink!

'Stop arguing, you two.' Mum placed her hand on Bertie's forehead. 'The priority must be to get the children to safety. Kevin, I'll take Bertie on Estella, if you please. He's burning up.'

Bertie slipped his hand into Mum's. He was unusually quiet. Hopefully, it was just the shock of it all.

'Of course, 'Phia. But remember she's prone to bucking.'

'I'm perfectly capable of riding a unicorn. You just concern yourself with getting Avariella and her little friend home. And don't forget poor Doreen. Thank goodness for the bumper crop of wart blossom this year.'

Mum climbed on to Estella. The unicorn threw her head back, trotting nervously from side to side, but grew calm again when Mum whispered softly into her ear.

'Still got it.' She winked at Kevin. 'I think you're forgetting, I was a dab hand with a unicorn back in the day.'

'Back in the day?' *This was getting weirder and weirder.*

'Yes, back in the day when I led the Protectors, sweetie. You're not the only princess who was destined to kick butt!'

# CHAPTER 41

Trumpets . . . ? An ogre blowing its nose . . . ? Alun flying outside my window . . . ? No, it was definitely trumpets I could hear. I jumped out of bed and threw back the curtains.

I shut them again.

Oh.

My.

Giddy.

Goblin.

There were people everywhere. The courtyard was, like, totally rammed. Holding my breath, I stepped closer to the window, my toes creeping under the soft velvet hem of the drapes. I eased them open and peeped through. Galloping unicorns, I didn't just dream it. This was really happening.

The bedroom door sprang open and Mum bounded into the room. She was wearing jeans and a silver tracksuit top like Kevin's. Mmm, I wasn't sure if it was cool or embarrassing... but it was definitely an improvement on the Little Bo Peep dress.

'My brave, amazing girl,' she said, throwing her arms around me and squeezing me with the force of an extremely hungry cobra.

I fought myself free from her suffocating grip, and she put her hands around her mouth like a megaphone.

'Flo!!!' she called.

*And, like, I'm uncouth, Dad!*

Flo, Mum's lady-in waiting, appeared holding a shiny purple dress I'd never seen before and never wanted to see again. She was followed by Jeb, who was wearing a satin onesie that matched the dress. He licked me, then threw himself down on the rug and started chewing the cuff of his trouser leg.

'Not that, silly billy,' Mum said, shaking her head at Flo. 'The bag. The bag.'

'Sorry, ma'am.' Flo hung the purple dress on the clothes rail. She disappeared again and came back with an oversized paper bag.

'Go on,' Mum said.

I reached inside the bag and took out the silver tracksuit top. Like, wowzas. It was the same as Mum's except it had a turquoise number one on the back. There were some jeans too and a stretchy T-shirt.

'Come on, Ava, hurry.' Mum grabbed the hem of my nightie and pulled it up over my head.

Normally, this would have annoyed me big-style. I mean, I'm old enough to dress myself. But given the cool clothes, I kept my gob shut and let her help me.

'Wow, you look amazing.' She took the platinum-handled brush off the dresser and brushed my hair into a sporty ponytail. I stared at my reflection in the mirror. What was Dad going to say?

Mum gave my ponytail a final tweak and opened the bedroom door. 'Now hurry, your people are waiting. You too, Sir Jeffrey.'

I picked up Jeb and followed Mum along the corridor, pausing at the family portrait that was painted just before I was born. Grandad George stared down at me, his eyes smiling. How could Odette do that, turn against her own family? Why did she want to bring darkness to Biscotti?

Mum put her hands on my shoulders. She kissed the top of my head. 'Grandad would have been so proud of you. He was devastated when Odette turned to the darkness. He blamed himself.'

I felt a warm feeling in my tummy. Me and Mum, talking properly.

'But why?'

'Because it was Grandad who reopened the portals after they'd been closed for hundreds of years. He was desperate to find a reason for Odette's evil streak – he pinned it on the Other

World, convincing himself it was the greed and materialism that had corrupted her.'

'And was it?'

The sadness in Mum's voice turned to anger. 'You've met her, right? Evil to the core. Even as a child she was dangerous and unpredictable. Grandad put it down to clumsiness at first – boiling her fish, frazzling her hamster – she was young, she hadn't taken control of her powers. But as she grew older, he could deny it no longer. He finally saw what everyone else saw: Odette enjoyed being evil.'

A cold chill ran down my spine. I curled a lock of Jeb's fur around my finger and hugged him tight. Mum was right. The way Odette had bounced up and down on her toes after she'd nearly drowned me, she was having an ace time. And she was so confident, free like nothing could stop her. Just like I felt when I was on a BMX. Maybe we were alike in some ways – some.

'No,' Mum continued. 'Odette could never take the throne. But when Grandad told her that, she decided to take it for herself. And she'd do anything to get it. You've seen what she did to Maude when she refused to help with her plans for world domination.'

I still couldn't believe what Odette had done to Aunt Maude: frying her brain, she'd called it. No wonder Maude was so frightened when we talked about *the one they sent away*.

Mum sighed and took my hand. She squeezed it gently. 'Grandad was never the same either. Only it was his broken heart that never recovered. Your father took over the throne and had no choice but to banish Odette.'

I felt suddenly cold. Bertie was safe, but I knew this wasn't the end of it. Odette was not going to just disappear. She wanted her throne back.

'Come now, my little fluff-louse.' Mum ran her finger gently over my cheek, wiping away the tears. How could I have been so wrong about her? There was so much more to Mum than the right royal fashion disaster I'd taken her for.

And there was more to me too. I just hoped Dad could see it.

I'd soon find out.

# CHAPTER 42

Dad was waiting with Bertie near the gold-embossed doors that opened out on to the balcony. Ooh, sunglasses please – Bertie's neon-orange knickerbocker suit could have lit up a small village. You'd have thought he'd want to avoid orange after the struggle the Godfather had reversing Odette's pumpkin-head charm, but apparently not.

He nudged Dad, who was busy helping Periwinkle wrestle Doreen's jaws from an oversized potted fern. *Yay!* The Godfather was right about her being back to normal in no time. Sure, she was a bit grey and one of her legs was shorter than the others, but she was still Doreen. I leant close to Mum, waiting for Dad's reaction to my tracksuit, but there was no disapproving look or lecture, just a smile and a kiss. My heart did a front flip flair– perhaps he really did mean what he'd said last night? Perhaps Dad really *was* proud of me.

'Good morning, Avariella,' he said, 'are you ready?' He took Jeb from me and gave him to Mum. 'The doors please, Periwinkle.'

The noise hit me like a snowboarding yeti. *Sensory overload or what!* Half of Biscotti was there – clapping, cheering and calling my name, their colourful silk flags and streamers dancing in the gentle, chocolate-scented breeze. Like any chance of me getting my mitts on some of that chocolate eggnog?

I waved – a proper wave, not one of those half-hearted princess jobbies that makes it look like you can't be bothered – and the cheering grew louder. So I waved again, this time with two hands. And I kept waving until the trumpeteers trumpeted their dragon-fart tune again.

'Thank you, citizens,' Dad said to the now silent crowd. He nodded at Periwinkle, who picked up a red velvet cushion. On the cushion there was a helmet – a silver helmet with a giant P on it, just like the emblem on my tracksuit and bike pump. My knees went all wobbly.

Dad picked up the helmet. He held it up to the crowd. Hushed whispers bounced around the courtyard. Nobody had a clue what was going on. Dad waited until everyone was quiet again. He smiled at me – I mean, twice in one day – and placed the helmet on my head.

'Proud citizens,' he said. 'I present Princess Ava, Prima Protector of Biscotti.'

The whispers were replaced by silence. People shook their heads and scratched their chins, wondering what the jumping jelly beans was happening. I couldn't blame them. I'd struggled to believe it too. But finding the portal, discovering BMX, it turns out it had all happened for a reason. I may not have magic like my aunties, but I had something that was perhaps more important. Just like Mum before me, I was one of the few who could harness the energy of the bluestone. And that meant I was duty-bound to protect my homeland.

'Think of the stone as a kind of thermostat,' Kevin had said on the way home last night. 'Some people aren't cut out to manage the gifts they're blessed with. They want power and use their magic in the wrong way. This disturbs the energy in the kingdom. The bluestone gets wise and seeks to return the balance – it wants to protect the groovy world it created. That's where the Protectors step in. They sort out whatever evil shenanigans the knights can't deal with and turn the thermostat back down.'

I thought Kevin was winding me up at first.

'Then why haven't I ever met one of these Protectors? Surely, they'd report to Dad.'

'Because they haven't been needed. Yer old man packed all the troublemakers off to the Other World. For years, we've only had minor problems like ogres and giants getting a bit out of hand – things even that mummy's boy Louseylot can deal with. But now Odette's found a way back to Biscotti, so can the rest of them. The bluestone is once again out of balance. It has chosen you to reform the Protectors and lead the battle to secure harmony.'

Ha! Kevin had obviously had one too many chai lattes. I mean, *me*, chosen by a mystical force to guard Biscotti; next he'd be suggesting there was no such thing as the Jelly Bean Pixie.

But the more I thought about it, on our journey back from the cornfields, the more Kevin's nonsense made sense. There had to be a reason for all of this. And there was definitely something weird going on with my bike pump. By the time we'd made it home, and packed Ethan off safely through the portal, he'd convinced me. But I didn't believe he'd ever convince Dad.

But now there Dad was telling the whole kingdom – I was the first of the new generation of Protectors.

'Yes,' he said. 'It is time to bring back the Protectors. For too long I have tried to shut out the past, believing this was the best way to keep you safe. If I denied the evil that once dwelt in Biscotti and erased it from our collective memory it could no longer haunt us.'

Dad went all amateur dramatics. He put his hand on his chest and looked out at the crowd, pleading.

'Forgive me, citizens, for I was wrong. Darkness has returned to Biscotti – and so must the Protectors.'

# CHAPTER 43

The cheering went on for, like, ever. Honestly, the crowd were showing me the love big-style. It would have been easy to get all big-headed, and go parade around on my bike or something, but that just wouldn't do. *A princess is not expected to bask in her own glory* – even if she is a radical, butt-kicking princess who rides a BMX.

'Oh, look!' Mum grabbed my arm. 'There's Nigel. Doesn't he look fantastic in his new boilersuit?'

*Eugh!* Mum was almost as bonkers as Odette.

Nigel – his boilersuit identical to his usual tinfoil babygro – cupped his hands around his mouth and shouted up to Mum.

Mum put the wriggling Jeb down on the floor and leant further over the stone wall. 'I'm afraid I can't hear you, poppet.'

The Godfather huffed and took his wand out. He shut his eyes and waved it above his head dramatically. There was a flash, followed by a low hum, and the crowd stood still as gargoyles.

'We're ready, Queenie.'

'Really, Nigel!' Dad said. 'Release the crowd from your spell. Let the girl have her moment.'

'Oh, Maggot 'ill have her moment, all right. Queenie and me 'ave got a little surprise for her.'

The Godfather climbed on to the platform used for public announcements. He waved his wand over the crowd. 'Right, you lot,' he said. 'Round the back. Show's not over yet.'

'Honestly,' Dad said, all red and shiny-faced, 'how many times have I told him, no magic unless it's an emergency?'

'Oh, don't be a spoilsport.' Mum's jaw tightened. 'What's the point in magic if you can't have a little fun from time to time?'

Mum led us downstairs and through the castle to the side door by the kitchens. Undoing the zip on her tracksuit top, she skipped outside into the sunlight. Jeb and Doreen followed, nipping at each other's ankles. Like, oh my giddy goblin, was that who I thought it was . . . ? *Was it!*

No way are you going to believe this, but there, perched on top of the hill, was Ethan. Ethan on his BMX, his front wheel pressed up against a full-size starting gate just like the one at Leanne Valley. Weirder still, lined up in the gate next to him, his Mohican poking through the slit in his studded bike helmet, was Kevin. The banner over their heads said: *Biscotti BMX Bonanza.*

I darted towards them, but Mum grabbed my hand.

'So, what do you think?'

What did I think? I threw my arms around Mum and gave her a taste of her own cobra-hug medicine. I mean, it was the sickest thing ever. My very own BMX track right here in Biscotti. Running straight down the hill, it twisted its way through the rose gardens and across the lawns, circling Aunt Maude's caravan before looping around the boating lake and winding its way back towards the castle. *Radical!*

Bertie wasn't quite so impressed. 'Oh my word,' he said, pushing his fringe out of his eyes. 'What is that monstrosity?'

'How in the name of Biscotti would I know,' Dad said. 'I'm just the King after all.'

Ethan waved. I was so desperate to go and say hello.

'It's quite obvious what it is, Bertrand. Kevsie thought it would be nice for the people to see their Prima Protector in action.'

Kevin nodded in agreement. He raised his hand and did the peace sign.

'And we wanted to check out the boy. We've had our eye on him for a while now. All those millions of people living in the Other World, do you really think he found his way here by chance?'

'So Ethan's from Biscotti?' I said.

'Don't be such a potato head. Of course not. But there's something connecting him with the bluestone. Kevin's certain. His crystals are never wrong.'

'Never,' confirmed Kevin, polishing his sunglasses.

'We're hoping to find a role for him. He's a bit of a wuss, but he did come good with the dragon and you can't do this all by yourself, Avariella. You need to build your front-line team as soon as possible. There are evil shenanigans breaking out left right and centre.'

Dad huffed, steadying himself against the castle wall as Jeb and Doreen rushed past and ran towards Kevin. 'The race, Sophia. The people are waiting.'

'Oh, yes. Now, where's Flo . . . ? *Flo!*'

'Yes, Your Highness.'

*Ooh, my bike, my bike. My lovely lovely bike.*

'Nigel's made a few alterations,' Mum said. 'I think you'll like them.'

'Nigel?'

'Yes, that's me name, don't wear it out.' The Godfather forced the wheel of his lime-green BMX between myself and Mum. The seat of his bike was covered in the same fluffy fur as his collar. 'Now come 'ead, Maggot. Time to see something really radical.'

# CHAPTER 44

The trumpeteer trumpeted his trumpety trump and the crowd grew silent. I shimmied into the start gate next to Ethan. He still had sherbet in his hair. It glistened in the sunlight.

'Shut it, you two,' said the Godfather, even though we hadn't said a word. 'I'm getting into the zone.'

Kevin smirked, the matchstick he was chewing on pointing upwards.

'Take your marks . . .' Mum waved her silk hanky.

'Get set . . .'

'*Go!*'

The gate fell.

So did the Godfather.

Seriously, he'd only just crossed the start line when I heard the screech of brakes and a thud behind me. So much for the radical.

'Sweet baby squirrel,' he shouted, his cries following me down the hill.

Unlike the Godfather, Ethan had flown out of the gate. It just goes to show how doing battle with an EVIL sorceress can focus your brain. Although it didn't seem to have focused mine. Ethan was getting further and further ahead. He hit the first jump and leant forward, lifting his front wheel and flying into the air. The roar of the crowd vibrated in my chest. They were mad for BMX. I put my head down and powered over the jumps and into the berm, Kevin dangerously close to my back wheel.

Keeping low on the turn I allowed myself a quick look over my shoulder. In the distance, near the start gate, the Godfather was climbing back on to his BMX. Wow, I so never expected Nigel to be a good sport. *Nice one!* I turned into the rhythm section. Ethan was like totally killing it. He circled Aunt Maude's caravan and stormed towards the final straight, where Sir Louseylot and his decidedly grey knights lined both sides of the track. Seeing Ethan approach, they readied their spears, lifting them diagonally over the track to form a victory arch.

When Ethan suddenly slowed, they lowered them again, scanning the grounds for signs of a problem. The roar of the crowd faded to a low buzz – what was wrong?

'Come on, Ava.' Ethan reached for my hand. 'Let's do this together.'

The noise of the crowd grew louder with every turn of the pedals. Their scarves were going ballistic now, a whirling sea of colour lining the track. Ethan let go of my hand and, side by side, we prepared to cross the finish line, where Mum, Dad and Bertie watched from their thrones, Doreen bucking and kicking as she tried to get free of her lead, and Jeb sitting on my golden chair with his tongue hanging out.

*Like, what!* Even Cook looked excited. Huddling with the other cheering servants, she squeezed Periwinkle's arm and waved her pinny at me. Mademoiselle Hornet-Boules was as straight as ever, but I suppose you can't have everything.

'Watch yerself, Maggot.'

The Godfather's back wheel skimmed my bike helmet. Tiny green stars sparkled above my head.

'Nobody gets past old Nige.'

'Dude,' Ethan laughed. 'You're supposed to ride the bike, not fly it.'

'Said nowt about that in the rule book.' The Godfather waved his wand. 'Ready?'

A blue switch flashed on my handlebars. Ethan looked from me to the Godfather. His bike was flashing too.

'Three . . . two . . . one,' we counted down together, our fingers hovering over the blue switches as we whizzed across the finishing line. '*Go!*'

I gripped my handlebars tightly, the sudden

charge making my BMX wobble. Steady now, I twisted the rubber handgrips and shot into the air. Pausing to wave at Aunt Maude, who was on her deck wearing a tutu, I chased Ethan upwards until we were level with the tip of the North Tower, the crowd below little bigger than Bertie's tin soldiers.

'Scream if yer wanna go faster,' said the God-father, flipping his bike in a double somersault.

'Gnarly!' Ethan flew vertically into the air. He levelled his bike out, the second sun burning orange behind him, and kicked the back wheel, whirling the frame round in a high-speed spin.

'You'll do,' said the Godfather, nodding in

approval. 'Now the pair of yer, get your scrawny butts down to the control room, there's work to do.'

'The control room?' *What was he on about now?*

'Fun's over, Maggot. Me crystal gazer's beeping on overdrive. Which can only mean one thing – more evil shenanigans. Now move it the pair of yer, this is where it gets really extreme.'

*Really extreme?* I'd have a bit of that! Get your typewriter out, Mademoiselle Hornet-Boules, because it looked like being a princess had just become a lot more interesting. It was time to rewrite those expectations!

# ACKNOWLEDGEMENTS

When you don't know where to start, it makes sense to start at the beginning. So my first thank you must go to Joanie and Jim Lad, my lovely parents, who taught me to value creativity and to question my place in the world. The years of sparring and swapping rubbish jokes at the dinner table were most excellent training for this adventure. Big love also to my brother James (Snowy loved me more) and my wider family – aunties, uncles, cousins, in-laws and outlaws – I was lucky to grow up surrounded by so many loving and supportive people. There's a little bit of all of you in this book.

Next up, then, is my lovely husband, who goes by many names but for the purpose of this book shall be known as Mark. Thank you for not laughing at me when I told you I was going to give up my job and write a book. And thanks for not crying when I then decided to do an MA in Creative Writing and leave the bill-paying to you for a bit longer. My greatest supporter and advocate, you never doubted me and I love you more than I'm prepared to say in this book. I don't want readers thinking I'm a soppy knickers now, do I?

Then there's my muse: the one and only Dylan James. With his harsh critique, invaluable wisdom and amazing knack for names, he is truly inspirational and only ever talked of *when* I'd be published – there was no *if* for my son Dylan. Thank you Dyl for being the most amazing champion any writer could have. I love you more than Frost's sausages cooked on the barbecue at the beach. (Oops, did I really say that out loud?)

On, then, to my writing friends. First up are the Manchees. I knew nothing about writing when I met these guys, but my MA buddies never let on I was rubbish. I couldn't have wished for a more supportive and lovely bunch of people to share the early part of my writing journey with. Funny, charming, generous and talented: I wish our salad days could have lasted for ever. Thanks also to the staff at MMU for their support and guidance. Special shout out to

Claudia Conerney and Kaye Tew who have created no end of opportunities and talked me up nearly as much as my mum.

And then there's the wonderful world of SCBWI. I can't thank my North West Network buddies enough – I'd never have done this without you. Thanks also to all the other Scoobies who've supported me along the way and made me believe I could do this. Particular thanks to the volunteers who make SCBWI British Isles the fantastic organisation it is – you got all the tricks!

It was through SCBWI I met Tilda Johnson, who reviewed the opening chapters of *Princess BMX* and encouraged me to keep going when I was convinced my manuscript was complete pants. Thank you, Tilda, for helping me keep the faith and for putting me in touch with my wonderful agent Kate Shaw who was, as you suggested, the perfect agent for me and Princess Ava. With her amazing ability to know exactly when I need a pep talk, and to say just the right thing, I'm certain Kate is of magical descent. My bet is on pixie princess – must check her ears out next time I see her. Thank you so much, Kate, for your support and magical prowess.

Talking of mythical creatures, like, how awesome is my editor Rachel Leyshon?! Rachel, I feel it was our destiny to come together so that we might give life to Doreen and Tyson and I could make you happy by signing off my emails *Two Ronnies* style. I have LOVED working with you. Thank you for seeing something shiny in my manuscript and polishing it until it truly sparkled. You were right about everything. Well, almost everything.

Thanks also to Barry Cunningham and Kesia Lupo who also championed *Princess BMX* from the start and welcomed me to the coop. I am truly grateful for the risk Chicken House took with a slightly wobbly BMXing princess and I couldn't have found a better home. A huge thank you to everyone in the Chicken House team who has played a part in making this book happen: Rachel Hickman, Elinor Bagenal, Laura Myers, Jazz Bartlett, Laura Smythe, Lucy Horrocks,

Sarah Wilson, you have all been so supportive and great to work with. How can so many truly lovely and dedicated people all work on the same team? Does Barry clone you?

If so, maybe he should clone illustrator Flavia Sorrentino because as far as I am concerned the world cannot get enough of her amazing illustrations. Thanks so much, Flavia, for bringing Biscotti and the cast of *Princess BMX* alive. I hope we get to have that hug sometime. Thanks also to designer Helen Crawford-White and copy-editor Sue Cook.

And, of course, thanks to all the friends and the new family members, I have gathered along the way, who have cheered me on from the sidelines. I wish I had room to mention everyone who has supported or inspired me, but you know who you are and I love you all. Special thanks, though, must go to my BMX gurus, Louis and Tania, and to Susan Kirkcaldy and Pam Smith who were my career gurus. Without Pam and Susan I might never have dared risk redundancy and follow my dreams.

And, finally, thanks to every radical BMXing prince or princess who has inspired this book, and to you, dear reader, for coming along on the ride. I hope you've enjoyed it.

A Swan House Ballet School Mystery

PERIL en POINTE

Helen Lipscombe

**PERIL EN POINTE by HELEN LIPSCOMBE**

Milly's in trouble. Moments after messing up the most important dance of her life, her prima ballerina mother vanishes. And that's just the beginning.

Out of the blue, Milly is invited to join a mysterious ballet school. But Swan House isn't just a school for ballet dancers. It's a school for spies.

Milly learns that she and her mother are in terrible danger. But has she got what it takes to face peril *en pointe*?

Paperback, ISBN 978-1-910655-79-5, £6.99  •  ebook, ISBN 978-1-912626-27-4, £6.99

## WHO LET THE GODS OUT? by MAZ EVANS

When Elliot wished upon a star, he didn't expect a constellation to crash into his dung heap. Virgo thinks she's perfect. Elliot doesn't. Together they release Thanatos, evil Daemon of Death. Epic fail.

The need the King of the Gods and his noble steed. They get a chubby Zeus and his high horse Pegasus.

Are the Gods really ready to save the world? And is the world really ready for the Gods?

*. . . lashings of adventure, the Olympic gods as you've never seen them before and a wonderfully British sense of humour.*
FIONA NOBLE, THE BOOKSELLER

Paperback, ISBN 978-1-910655-41-2, £6.99 • ebook, ISBN 978-1-910655-64-1, £6.99

## THE GREAT CHOCOPLOT by CHRIS CALLAGHAN

It's the end of chocolate – for good! A chocolate mystery...
At least that's what they're saying on TV.

Jelly and her gran are gobsmacked – they love a Blocka
Choca bar or two.

But then a train of clues leads back to a posh chocolate shop
in town owned by the distinctly bitter Garibaldi Chocolati.

Is it really the chocopocalypse, or a chocoplot to be cracked?

With an excellent cast of characters, laugh-out-loud
moments, and witty and sharp observations, this
is a great choice for fans of Dahl and Walliams.
GUARDIAN

Paperback, ISBN 978-1-910002-51-3, £6.99 • ebook, ISBN 978 -1-910655-57-3, £6.99